HER WOLF

THE WESTERVELT WOLVES BOOK 1

REBECCA ROYCE

Published 2011
ISBN-13: 978-1456568382
ISBN-10: 1456568388

Copyright © 2011, Rebecca Royce. All rights reserved. No part of this publication may be reproduced, stored in a retrieval system, or transmitted in any form or by any means, electronic, mechanical, recording or otherwise, without the prior written permission of the author.

Manufactured in the United States of America

Cover Art and Book Design: April Martinez

Chapter One

Ashlee Morrison automatically searched for him in the crowd. When she found him, she stopped breathing for a second as pleasure swirled within her chest. With his dark mane and his proud posture, he would have stood out even if he didn't avoid the others. She walked closer, just to the edge of where he was visible to her, careful not to draw attention to herself.

Loneliness hung like a tangible cloak around him. Ashlee chuckled at her crazy thoughts. God, if anyone heard her inner dialogue, they'd think she was talking about a man, not a wolf.

She strolled around the outskirts of the Polloza Park and Zoo's large wolf enclosure and stopped every few feet to look through the fence. In the last week, the wolves had started playing together like puppies. They ran after one another, the bigger ones pounced on top of the smaller ones as they nipped and bit. It wasn't really play—she knew that—it was all about getting the attention of one of the females who was in heat. That's what the zoologists explained to her yesterday when she'd asked about the strange pack behavior. Well, it seemed strange to her anyway.

But who was she to judge anything as odd or different? If she hadn't literally lost her mind and started ranting about impossible scenarios to anyone who would listen, she would now be finished with college and not living at back at home with her mother and father. She'd have a real job instead of her volunteer one at the local zoo. The doctors her father had taken her to see had helped her. She could finally tell the difference between real and imaginary.

Real was day-to-day life. Work, family, and friends were the things she needed to focus on. They actually existed. Neurotic daydreams of her sister being locked up in a cage were nothing more than manifestations by inner psyche that was still devastated by Tom's betrayal. Coupled by the internal jealousy the doctors insisted she had towards her sister was evidently, in Ashlee's head, a recipe for disaster. Even if she had never been aware of any green-eyed feelings towards Summer before the episode six months ago. She believed the psychiatrists; if they said she was envious, she wasn't really in any position to argue with them. They were highly sought after professionals and, to Ashlee's relief, at the last session they had told her family she was doing better.

Which was exactly why she didn't tell anyone about the feelings of claustrophobia that nearly overwhelmed her each time she got too close to the wolf cage or about the strange male voice she heard in her head on an almost daily basis now.

A stab of pain pierced her stomach and she pressed her hand there. Nothing like hunger to take her out of her inner musings and back to reality. She needed to stay in the here-and-now and, moreover, she shouldn't have skipped lunch. At least her appetite had returned, that must mean she was getting back to normal. She leaned against the outside wall of the enclosure and tried to enjoy nature's mating show.

Not all of the pack joined in the fun. "The lone wolf" as she had come to think of him did not seem in the least bit interested in the pack's antics. In fact, he looked bored. The others avoided him as if he was diseased. Maybe he was. Didn't animals know when one of their kind was sick and avoided them? Even kill the one who was unwell? Was that true for pack animals? She wasn't an animal expert, just a volunteer whose job was to point the visitors towards the gift shop or the restroom if they asked for it.

The thought of him being ostracized, or worse, put down, made her sad but she shoved it away. Sad thoughts were not allowed to form in her mind; they got out of control in there. She pulled her olive green fleece volunteer jacket tighter around her to protect against the cold fall breeze. For some reason over the last few months she'd come to think of him as hers, which was stupid, of course, but she'd adopted him in her heart anyway. Even convinced herself that it was her voice she could hear. His intonations that watched her walk and worried about her health and well being while ranting about being locked up and betrayed. Ashlee supposed it could be worse. Her delusions were at least kind to her and concerned for her welfare. They weren't asking her to shave her head or kill anyone.

A woman pulled on her sleeve and caught her attention. "Excuse me, miss, which way is the restroom? My son's had an accident."

Ashlee looked at the mother and her little boy. Thirty-five, maybe older with brown hair that already held some grey. She guessed the boy was around three years old. She noted his Halloween costume—a pumpkin—had a urine stain down the front. Ashlee smiled at his big round face and dimpled cheeks.

"Straight down that path and to the left." She hoped she didn't look sad. Cute kid.

"Thank you, pretty lady." The three-year-old boy gave her a big grin and pulled his mother toward the bathroom path.

Pretty lady? Not lately. Twenty-two years old and so tired, she could barely see straight. Her red hair, once strawberry blonde, seemed to have dulled along with her brain. With bland green eyes, pale skin, and a figure that needed another ten pounds to be curvy, she wound up looking sick, instead of slender.

She cleared her throat and looked at the wolf. These days all she needed were those brief glances to feel content, another fact she kept from her team of psychiatrists.

Her father had signed her on for this job even as she sobbed in her bed every day. He'd thought it would get her mind off Tom and keep her from having another incident. He was right. Her summer volunteer position had extended into the fall, and now two weeks from Halloween, she hadn't earned a dime, but she no longer mourned the five year relationship that had ended so badly. More importantly, she wasn't having any more strange manifestations of impending doom. She assumed Tom had married the mother of his almost-time-to-be-born child by now.

Ashlee shrugged and let the memories fade. She walked to the gate of the wolf pen and stared in. Usually, she didn't get close to the animal cages; it felt invasive to do so and sometimes she would swear it felt like she was personally trapped in the cage. The animals spent all day with people pushed up against their enclosures pointing and staring. She preferred to give them some space. She blinked and squinted. The lone-wolf had red fur in its coat. Why hadn't she noticed that before? Because she hadn't been able to focus on anything before and she was going out of her way to not spend too much time focused on the lone wolf.

Her Wolf

Ashlee smiled, and the wolf raised its eyes to look at her. She blushed, which made her feel ridiculous. He was a wolf, for god's sake, but his eyes looked so human, so compassionate. That compassion drew her in. She leaned closer to the cage. She snorted. For the last ten minutes, she'd done nothing but personify animals. Talk about desperate. Maybe it was time to go back to school.

"Can't be fun for you to be so alone in there. Maybe you would have been happier with a different pack." She'd just broken her cardinal rule and spoken to the animal. She closed her eyes at the slip-up.

Ha! Not this pack, that's for sure. My family actually walks on two legs some of the time. I'd love to take you to meet them. I bet if I got you there, you might actually smile. I hate that half-grimace thing you seem so fond of.

Ashlee jumped back from the enclosure, so startled she fell on her behind. Had the wolf just talked to her in her mind or had her hallucinations gotten worse? She stood and looked around her. Her cheeks burned. No patrons or other volunteers were about to see to see her act like a lunatic, which was fortuitous or she'd soon be fired from her volunteer position.

She cleared her throat and looked around again. No one nearby, just the trees with their colored leaves, the wind, and the wolves. Her butt hurt from her earlier fall. She narrowed her eyes to stare at the wolf. "Did you say something?" She groaned. Why was she playing into this? You don't talk to figments of your imagination.

Did you hear me, little one? The wolf's ears perked up, and he stood up on all fours to walk towards the side of the enclosure she pressed against. *Is it possible you have been here with me all this time and you can actually hear me? Why have you not answered me before?*

She should put a stop to this right now and walk away. But, she didn't. Her feet felt glued to where they stood on the ground. She felt a light wind pick up and blow her hair off her shoulders. Not knowing what else to do, she swallowed the nervous bile that had formed in her throat. "I don't know how I hear you, but yes, I can. Unless I've cracked up, which is most likely what's going on here. That's why I don't answer you. I don't want to be crazy anymore."

Crazy? You haven't cracked up. Perhaps I have. Her wolf sniffed the air and walked closer. He howled and Ashlee took a step backwards. *That smell. Your scent. I know it. You never get close enough to let me smell you. The spell, it must have limited my other powers. My sense of smell is worse than some humans. Could it be?*

Ashlee's heart pounded in her chest. "Wow, we're really having a conversation, aren't we?"

You…you are…mine.

She looked around again to be sure that no one approached. "What does that mean?"

How could you be here so often, for so long, and I did not know? I will kill Rex and any others who inflicted this intolerable state upon me.

Kill? Ashlee's pulse sped up. Her palms grew sweaty and she wiped them on her pants. "I'm sorry, I've got to go."

No, no little one, you cannot leave me in this pen. You must get me out and return with me to my home where my pack can restore me. I need to tell my family about the one who has betrayed us.

"Get you out of the cage? Are you nuts? See, I knew it was just a matter of time before my delusions wanted me to do something that was against the law. No. I'm in charge of my own mind. I get to say what I will and won't do. This whole thing goes so far beyond the realm of normal I can't even see the border anymore. I can't get you out of the cage. I can't let a wolf run around the park where there are children. They'll lock me up and shoot you."

I would never hurt a child. But you still believe I am a mere animal and for some reason you think you are not mentally well. Not until I return home can I show you otherwise. The wolf lay down on his belly. His head pressed to the ground. *Damn.*

Ashlee's eyes filled with tears at the distress in his voice and the defeat in his body language. It had been a few weeks since she'd gone on a crying binge and she didn't want to start now. "I have to go. I'm sorry." Why was she apologizing to her phantasm? She wiped the one tear that escaped from her eye with her hand and turned to go.

Wait. Her wolf growled and stood up. Ashlee turned back to him, her eyes wide. *Do not cry. I cannot stand it. Please, beautiful girl, won't you tell me your name?*

"My name? Oh." She blushed. "My name is Ashlee

Morrison." She started to leave again but whirled around. "What is your name?" At least she could give her delirium a label.

My name is Tristan Kane. My family calls me Trip.

She raised her eyebrow. They'd had a kid in her high school who had been called Trip. She hadn't realized it was such a popular nickname. "You have a beautiful name like Tristan and they call you Trip? Hey, wait a second, a guy I knew with that nickname, they called him that for a reason. He was the third son in his family. Is that true for you? Are you the third son?"

I am. I'm sorry I am moping around. Five months I have been in this cage. Please don't worry about this tonight. We can sort it out tomorrow when you come.

She shook her head. "I'm not coming tomorrow. It's my day off, and then the next day is Sunday so I won't be back until Monday."

That long? Tristan shook his head. *Do not worry for me. I will not have you upset. Ashlee whatever you do, don't let anyone tell you this isn't real. What is happening is very complicated, but explainable just the same. I am real and you can hear me because you belong to me.*

Ashlee turned and ran as if someone chased her. She didn't turn around to look at Tristan. When she reached her black Lexus RX hybrid SUV, she swung open the door and drove her monstrous car as if her life depended on it. What should have been a fifteen-minute drive home, she made in less than five minutes. It wasn't 'til she got home she remembered her shift wasn't over for another hour. She was sure to get a stern lecture.

Tristan paced the pen for maybe the thirtieth time that evening. How could his mate have been standing outside this godforsaken cage for five months without him smelling her? It was the spell. That had to be the reason. Traitorous Rex had trapped him in this form and taken away all of his extrasensory abilities, which now made him the weakest, most pathetic wolf in existence.

A wolf trapped with human senses. What kind of wolf-shifter didn't automatically recognize their mate? He sighed in frustration. If he'd been in his human form he would have pounded on something. But since his only options for her relief were the non-shifter wolves in the cage with him, he was out of luck for stress relief partners.

His mate. But God she was beautiful. *Ashlee.* He'd watched her for months now. Every week wasting away and, truthfully, he worried for her health and before today it had concerned him that he'd been so obsessed with her. Now, at least, his level of interest made sense. Was she unwell? The healers could fix it, whatever it was. She was Wolf, even though she didn't know it yet. The pieces were finally fitting together. She was the right age. She must have been sent away for protection. His pack had come to believe all their females were dead. But, his mate lived. It was too extraordinary to believe.

He would convince her to let him out and then he would take her home. She was so young, but she was his. As soon as he got out of this zoo, he would guard her until he had no breath left in him. His body shook at the thought. If he lived another hundred years, no one would ever cage him again or keep him from Ashlee.

Ashlee struggled to wake. She opened her eyes and tried to calm her breathing. Her heart pounded hard in her chest and tears fell down her cheeks. Tristan, her wolf. She'd dreamt of him. Not dreamt, she corrected herself, she'd had another episode and this time it hadn't been about her sister Summer, it was Tristan who had featured in it. But he hadn't looked like a wolf— no he'd been a man, but she had known it was him. Tall, with brown hair that held specks of red in it. His nose long and regal, bordered by cheekbones a GQ model would envy. He had a five o'clock shadow across his chin. His brown eyes were hooded and sad. Men were on their way for him, the men who had trapped him in his wolf form, and they would kill him if they found him. They would finish the job they'd started months ago.

How did she know this? The dream or hallucination or whatever it was had seemed so real. No, she corrected herself, it didn't just *seem* real, it was real. Tristan had insisted she wasn't crazy. But wasn't that just what a senseless illusion would say? Ashlee closed her eyes against the conflict that raged in her head. There were two options. Either she needed to be institutionalized and watched by professional doctors who could help her sort out real from imaginary or she was sane and all of this was really happening. Did mentally ill patients know they were not well? Didn't the very fact that she questioned what was happening to her mean she was still able to tell what was true and what was not?

She opened her eyes. She needed to make a decision about this immediately. If there were men after Tristan then she was running out of time.

Ashlee didn't hear any noises in the house; her parents weren't back from their evening out yet. They were out at a gala where her father was receiving yet another award. He was the head of plastic surgery at their local hospital. She wasn't sure where he got the time to do all the things that he did. He devoted hours to pro bono surgeries that helped restore the facial features of burn victims. It was nice that he was getting recognized but she really could have used her mother's advice and she couldn't help but wish they had gotten home already. Her mother would know what to do and, ironically, Ashlee wasn't sure that Victoria Morrison would doubt her sanity.

An image from her childhood swirled into her mind, taking over and for a moment Ashlee felt like she was there again. She'd sat on the bed, eight years old, while Victoria brushed her long strawberry blond hair. Summer lay next to her, blonde and blue eyed like Victoria, almost their mother's perfect copy. Ashlee had felt disturbed by the horror movie they'd watched--or at least she felt like she should have been bothered by the graphic images, since all of the other girls at the sleepover had been scared. She asked her mother if there were such things as monsters.

Victoria had paused the brush mid-stroke and looked down at her with a startled expression marring her otherwise perfect, Nordic features. She'd regained her composure quickly.

"Do *you* think there are monsters, Ash?"

Ashlee hadn't known what to say. Something about her mother's tone had made her more nervous than the monster movie with the chainsaw-wielding psycho killer. What was it? Thinking with her adult mind and not that of her younger self, Ashlee realized her mother had sounded anxious. Fourteen years later, Ashlee couldn't remember ever hearing Victoria sound quite like that again.

Summer had interrupted then; she was never satisfied until she had every answer she needed. "Do you, Mom? Do you believe?"

Ashlee thought she knew what her mom would say. It was the job of grownups to reassure you, to tell you that nothing scary was real.

"I do believe, girls. Some of the things that go bump in the night are real and we must always be on guard for them. But don't worry, nothing will ever harm you here while I am with you."

The memory, like dust in the sky, floated out of her mind and Ashlee was back in the present with her decision already made for her. Why wasn't it possible that Tristan could speak to her, even if he was a wolf? It wasn't any more unreasonable than anything else. People believed in ghosts and no one called them crazy. Hell, she'd had a friend whose mother attended conferences about aliens. Declaring herself a lunatic hadn't worked out so well, maybe it was time to try a different approach. Just for tonight, she would believe.

Tristan was a talking wolf and she was going to save him from the men who were out to get him.

She looked at her small black alarm clock on her nightstand. 10:30 PM. She'd only been asleep for an hour. Wearing her flannel red and black pajamas, Ashlee jumped from her bed and ran out of her bedroom. She didn't have time to change her clothes, the urgency to reach Tristan at the zoo too great. She rushed through the house pausing only to write her parents a note.

Mom and Dad, I may have gone off the deep end but there is a wolf that talks at the zoo. I know, I know. I'm nuts. But he needs me to break him out and I'm going to do it. If you need to call the doctors and send me away. I understand. I love you and I wish I didn't have to do this. But, I do, even though it makes no logical sense.

I love you. –Ash

She rushed into the garage. She grabbed the key off the wall where it hung and climbed into her SUV.

She pulled out of her driveway fast and rounded the corner down the suburban street. Her tires squealed and she forced herself to slow down. Jail…she might do hard time for this. She was going to break a wolf out of a government owned zoo. That meant it was a felony. She swallowed the saliva that pooled in her mouth and clenched her teeth together until they hurt. Too late to back out now. At least her parents could afford a good attorney when the police arrested her and they had her note to prove how out of her mind she really was.

She pulled into a parking space close to the employee gate—the zoo was empty of people, she had her pick— and rushed out of the car. Her key fit perfectly in the door and she stepped inside. Quickly, she plugged her code into the silent alarm. Its unique numbers would identify her to zoo security. They would know exactly who had broken out the wolf based on that alone. She sighed.

Quietly, she followed the path towards the wolves. The monkeys screeched when she passed them, but otherwise only the hiss of the dully-lit gas path lights acknowledged her arrival. She reached the pen and looked down. Tristan's ears shot upwards as he became alert and he stood to run towards the wall.

What are you doing here, my Ashlee?

She swallowed. She could still hear him. He was still a talking wolf. That hadn't changed. "I've had a dream."

A bad dream? He paced around in a circle in front of her.

"It felt very real to me. I'm getting you out before the men who did this to you arrive." She paused. "Some men did this to you, didn't they? Trapped you like this?"

That's correct. Do you have these psychic dreams often, little Ashlee?

She shook her head and walked towards the gate. "No. This was my first and hopefully my last."

It would be easy. She would let Tristan out, he would go wherever it was that he went, and then things could go back to normal. Assuming, that is, she didn't get caught in this jailbreak, which, of course she would, and also assuming her parents didn't lock her up and throw away the key.

"Tristan, I can't let the other wolves out. Unless they're also humans trapped as animals?"

Tristan snorted in what might have been something like a laugh. *No, they are wolves. They will not come near the gate.* He turned around, growled at the pack, and showed his teeth. His meaning was clear—back off.

Ashlee opened the door and Tristan trotted out. He sniffed the ground in front of him. Ashlee closed and locked the gate. Up close, Tristan was an even more impressive animal. Thick, brown fur with red patches, deep sunken brown eyes specked with grey, and filled with intelligence. Absentmindedly, she reached out to stroke his fur but jumped back when she caught herself. She sucked in a breath. It was one thing to contemplate breaking out a wolf, another thing to actually be alone with one, let alone touch it. Those teeth could take off her hand. She stepped backwards and hit the wall behind her hard.

Tristan followed her retreat and nudged her with his head until she touched him of her own volition.

With great trepidation, Ashlee petted Tristan on his head and then on his back and sides. He was coarse under her touch and he smelled clean, like the first scent of fresh air on an early summer morning. She laughed at the thought and he nudged her.

You must never fear me. I will never hurt you. Only to you will I ever make that promise.

"Come with me. We've got to get you out of here." She heard the click of the nails on his paws as he followed behind her. She ran towards the front gate. She looked around and opened it, noting the way the moonbeams played on the bars, giving it the impression of swimming in the moonlight. Tristan loped through the gateway and into the shadows.

Her breath shook in her throat. "So what happens now? Do you run home or something?" She didn't know what to do with her arms and legs. She felt lost in the space around her. How did you say goodbye to a magical talking wolf? For a moment, only silence met her query.

Ashlee, I cannot leave you. I am hopeful you will take me home to my pack and you will meet my family. But if you cannot, then I will stay with you.

She knew she shouldn't have just accepted all of this as commonplace, certainly it was weird, but if she was in for a penny, she was in for a pound. Weird prophetic dreams, talking wolves, shifters…why not? It felt right to her. In the same way that she knew she had red hair, she knew this was real. "You can't stay with me. Where would I put you? Besides, if you get home, they can help you, right? They can make it so you can be a man again?"

So that I can be a man when I choose to and a wolf when I want, yes. They can help me with this.

She blew out the breath she'd been unaware she held. "Then I guess I'll take you home. Where do you live?"

On an island, off the coast of Maine.

"An Island off the coast of Maine? We're in New Jersey. That's what eight, nine hours from here?" She shook her head. How would she explain where she'd gone? Her family would worry. She'd need a good excuse. Her parents had taken to treating her as if she were a child ever since her breakdown.

I would guess more like ten hours considering we will need to wait for the boat.

A really, really good excuse.

She walked towards her waiting SUV and popped open the door. "Hop in. I'll drive you to Maine, and then I'll turn around and come back. I can be back for dinner tomorrow night. I'll make up some excuse."

The wolf snorted. *You will not be back for dinner tomorrow night.*

She furrowed her brow at his authoritative tone. "Yes, I will."

Tristan remained silent. She narrowed her eyes and rubbed her nose. She knew she hadn't won the argument, he'd humored her. This day really wasn't going as planned. She turned to get into the car but stopped when she saw Tristan's head jerk upwards.

His nose moved frantically in the air as he sniffed something. He growled and she shuddered.

Her voice wavered. "Tristan?"

Get in the car, little one.

She followed his gaze and turned around. Behind her car, three men stepped out of the shadows. They were the men from her dream. She whirled around and stared at Tristan. His teeth flaunted, he growled loudly. Gone was her sweet, gentle wolf and in his place stood a terrifying animal. She had a feeling this situation called for just that kind of creature.

The first man stepped forward. His hair, long and blond, hung down his back. He turned in the light and she saw that half of his face was tattooed with the symbol of a serpent. "Hello, Tristan. We've been looking for you," the blond man lisped. He really sounded like a snake.

Tristan snarled and moved towards the snake man who turned around to smile at the other two would-be attackers, both dark haired. One of them was small in stature, the other the exact opposite, huge and built like a linebacker.

"Look boys, I don't think he can shift back yet. I think the beloved boy is still stuck." He laughed. "Classic." The other two men snickered. "Get the leash and catch his little girl before she runs."

Linebacker turned around to grab Ashlee. She didn't think, just reacted. She swung open the back door of her SUV as he stepped forward. It collided with the man's gigantic gut. He fell backwards a step. He made an *oomph* noise and stalked forward. Instinct made her run. She went no more than ten feet when her mind screamed for her to turn around and help Tristan.

A scream of agony cut through the night air as Tristan attacked Ashlee's pursuer. Her wolf went right for the giant man's throat. Tristan ripped and tore him to pieces as he bit and attacked the huge man with his teeth and claws. Blood splattered and coated Tristan's fur. The concrete beneath them turned red from the gaping wounds.

Ashlee tried not to gag and spun around in an attempt to avoid the scene as it unfolded. She lost her balance, tripped and hit the ground. She grunted as her shoulder took the brunt of her weight, followed immediately by her head as it hit the pavement. Her teeth tore into her tongue. She saw stars and spit out the blood that came from the bite she'd given her tongue.

The smaller attacker stood over her now. He reached down to grab her. Suddenly, he was down on the ground. Another wolf, not Tristan, attacked him as it literally ripped the skin from the man's face. The scream was short lived as only moments later the wolf locked onto his throat.

How hard had she hit her head? Where had this second wolf come from?

Unlike Tristan, this wolf was entirely black. The attacker reached into his belt for something hidden there. He pulled out a knife and struck the black wolf on his left shoulder. It was an act of desperation because Ashlee guessed the man was already on his way to death's door. The wolf whimpered for a moment, but didn't stop his assault as he shredded the hand that held the knife to nothing but bone.

Ashlee rolled onto her side and looked for Tristan. He growled and stalked the blond snake-man who held the leash he'd ordered the others to get. She'd seen this type of lead before. If Snake-boy managed to touch Tristan with the end of it, an electric shock would be released and render Tristan paralyzed for a moment. Enough time for him to be caught.

She had not gone through all the trouble of breaking Tristan out only to lose him to that electric stunner.

She crouched and her body screamed with pain. Fury filled her body and she smiled. Had she ever been this angry before? Before she could stand up a third wolf, this one small and white, leapt from the darkness onto Snake's back. He went down onto his belly. Tristan attacked from the other side as the white wolf finished him off from behind by ripping out his throat. Growls filled the air and drowned out the screams. Moments later, there was nothing but silence.

Ashlee's head spun. She sat back on her butt and touched her forehead. Blood stained her right hand when she pulled it back. She must have really gashed open her head. Gagging at the sight of her own blood, she looked at the ground to regain her equilibrium. Two bare feet obstructed her vision and she jerked her head upright to look. A man stood before her, completely nude. His hair was the same shade of black as the wolf who'd attacked the short assailant and saved her.

He knelt on the ground next to her. His hand pushed up against his shoulder to put pressure on a bleeding wound. This man was the black wolf. She'd thought she'd accepted the fantastical when she broke Tristan out of the wolf pen, but her stomach still rolled at the thought that this person and the wolf were the same being.

His eyebrows raised, he looked at her. "Are you hurt badly, ma'am?"

Ma'am? She had one second to register the man's kind voice in her brain before Tristan attacked him. Her wolf leapt into the air and toppled the stranger onto the ground. His teeth shown, he growled just as fiercely as he had at that their attackers. Tristan's face loomed over the stranger's only inches apart.

Ashlee staggered to her feet "Tristan, he saved me!"

He didn't struggle under Tristan's attack. The black haired stranger lay perfectly still. "It wasn't me, Trip. I swear it. I know you think it was, but I didn't do it. I got there too late. I swear it, brother. I've searched for you for six months. I didn't betray you to Father's men. I've been following them, looking for you." His voice sounded raw with emotion, Ashlee could hear him gasp as he tried to get enough air. "Rip out my throat brother, if you don't believe me. Rip it out."

Tristan stared down at his brother and stopped growling but didn't move from his attack posture.

"I saved your woman. She is yours, isn't she? I can smell it. Why would I save her if I wanted you dead?"

Tristan bowed his head and his brother took a deep

breath. Ashlee watched Tristan step off the other man's body and limp over towards her.

She gasped. "You're hurt?" She leaned down to touch his front paw. He yelped.

"Yes, they're both hurt. And it's exactly this kind of grandstanding that I haven't missed for the last thirty years."

Ashlee jerked her head around, her mouth dropped open. Her mother stood before her, completely naked. Suddenly embarrassed, Ashlee covered her eyes with her hand to not see her mother's nude form.

She swallowed and turned around so she couldn't see her mother. She opened her eyes. "Mom, what are you doing here? I mean…I can explain." She didn't know how she was going to explain, she'd already confessed her intentions in the note she'd left. Wait a minute, what was her mother doing there and why was she naked?

"No, Ashlee, I think I'm going to have to explain. When I got home I read your note and I could smell you fear all over the house so I followed the GPS signal your father had installed in your car." Her mother's voice sounded tired.

The GPS signal in her car? Why had her father felt the need to spy on her and what had her mother meant by smelled her fear? Ashlee opened her mouth to question her mother but Rex answered her first.

"Victoria?" Ashlee opened her eyes and saw Tristan's brother had stood up and walked towards Ashlee's mother, his hand on his shoulder again.

"It's me, Rex. Only everyone here calls me Vicki. I'm exhausted. I haven't been in wolf form in nearly two decades. Come. My mate is a surgeon, and he knows about all of this."

Tristan growled at that last statement.

"Oh hush it, Trip. Why would he expose us? He'd be dooming his own daughter if he did that."

Ashlee turned to look at her mother, her mouth hung open in disbelief. Her mother was also a wolf? What the heck was going on? Her mother stared at Ashlee, her mouth slightly ajar. "I knew you were extraordinary Ash, but I thought it was just a mother's pride talking. Never in a million years did I think you would end up the mate of one of the Royal Six."

Mate? "The what?"

Tristan nudged at her leg with his nose and she moved to the car.

She'll explain this to you when we get to your home. Or I will. Tristan's voice soothed Ashlee's strung out nerves.

Her mother turned to walk towards the darkness. "I'll take care of cleaning up this mess and I'll meet you back at home. Ashlee, take the princes back with you to our house." Ashlee nodded even though she doubted her mother could see her.

Her car door still hung open and despite his injured paw, Tristan leaped easily into the backseat. Ashlee closed the door behind him and got into the front. Rex, that's what her mother had called Tristan's black haired brother, climbed into the passenger front seat.

Ashlee handed Rex the emergency blanket her parents made her keep in the backseat. He wrapped himself up in it. Tristan growled.

Rex groaned. "Come on, Trip. I just got you back. I am certainly not making a play for your mate. She already shares your scent. She's yours. I get it. I'll climb in the back if it makes you more comfortable. "

Rex turned around in his seat, still holding his shoulder, and manipulated himself over the console to the backseat. Tristan climbed through the center and sat in the front passenger seat next to her. Ashlee, unable to resist the need, reached out and stroked his fur. He lay across the front seat, eyes upwards and gazed at her. She swallowed away the strange unknown feeling that had formed in her stomach.

She put the key in the ignition and started the car. Rex stretched out in the backseat and yawned before saying, "My brother isn't usually so possessive. But then again he's never been mated so maybe this is just how he is."

Can it, Rex.

Ashlee laughed and so did Rex. She pulled out of the zoo parking lot, leaving behind three dead bodies, all with their throats ripped out, and her alarm code plugged into the zoo security system to explain it. She was going to be in so much trouble.

"I'm going to get blamed for those bodies."

Rex leaned forward in the backseat. "I can hear your mother in her car. She's on the phone with some people who are going to handle this. You won't be in any trouble. Victoria appears to be a woman of influence, even in some less than upstanding circles." Rex paused. "Excuse me, miss, I'm sorry, I don't know your name."

Her name is Ashlee, pup. But I don't see why you need to use it.

Rex laughed again and then groaned. He grabbed his shoulder. "Because it's more polite than saying 'hey you'. Ashlee, do you think I could borrow your cell phone?"

"I don't have it with me. I ran out of the house in my pajamas." She took her eyes off the road and examined herself for a moment before she groaned at her appearance. She grimaced and returned her eyes to the dark road. "I have so many questions."

Of course you do.

She touched his head again. She wasn't usually this affectionate but she needed to touch Tristan. "Are you in much pain?"

He closed his eyes under her touch. *A bit.* Ashlee looked in the rearview mirror at Rex. His eyes stared out the window for a moment before he closed them. The two wolves in the car with her were exhausted. Two wolves. In the car. With her. Why did the nonsensical seem so okay?

And what had her mother meant by mate?

Chapter Two

Ashlee sat across from her father as he finished stitching Rex's shoulder. Tristan's brother, shirtless but clothed from the waist down, endured her father's ministrations without complaint.

When they arrived home, her dad had immediately gone to work on her, and sewn four neat stitches on her forehead. She had not behaved quite as stoically as Rex. Good thing her father was a plastic surgeon, or she might carry a really unpleasant scar for the rest of her life, a constant reminder of her evening. Not that it was likely she would ever forget it.

Her mother, who was now fully clothed, sat across from Tristan and wrapped his paw in a bandage. When she finished, she stood and surveyed the room in the way only her mother could. Ashlee had seen her do it a million times. It was as if she calculated the risk each person in the room presented to her. Now that she knew her mom could become a canine at will, her mother's actions made a lot more sense. Finally, when she was finished, she crossed the room to sit next to Ashlee.

"Okay, Ash, I'm going to try my best to explain…"

Ashlee cut in angrily, her words tinged with the outrage she felt. "Start with how you knew about all of this. Why you can turn into a wolf like Tristan and Rex and I didn't know about it. And why if you knew the impossible could be true, like say, that its possible for a person to have visions that might actually come true, why you let me think I was crazy for the last half of a year. How could you not tell me that those things I was seeing might actually be true?"

Her mother sighed and looked down for a moment. "It's all a very long story. But I guess to answer you last question first, your father and I let you think you were crazy because we hoped you were. You've never shown any wolf signs. I had no reason to believe you held the magic inside of you. The doctors said you were showing symptoms of post traumatic stress related to the ending of your engagement and I chose to believe that was true. I didn't want you mixed up in this in madness. I thought if I believed hard enough that you were a beautiful, smart, sensitive girl with no special abilities than that was what you would be. I owe you an apology. I'm sorry, my love."

Her mother's eyes had filled with tears that Ashlee watched her blink away. She wanted to reach up and touch her mother but she didn't. She was mad. Her parents, who knew it was possible she could have visions and exhibit out-of-the-ordinary behavior had let her think she was crazy because they were scared? It made sense but it infuriated her just the same. She gritted her teeth to keep from yelling. She knew better than to make a scene in front of strangers. It would only make the situation worse.

Her father spoke up, his brown eyes swimming. "That's why I sent you to the zoo, Ashlee. I thought maybe if you did have the gift than being around all of those animals might help you somehow."

"I tried to get him to change his mind. I was wrong again, if your dad hadn't sent you there, you never would have found Trip. I apologize again." Her mother looked at her hands.

Ashlee wanted to bang her head against the wall at the utter wrongness of this whole situation. "Okay. Enough apologies. What was done is over. I don't understand it, I may never. But it was a memory of you telling me monsters were real that convinced me to go and help Tristan tonight so ultimately you helped all of us, I guess. Please continue your story." She was surprised at how reasonable she sounded and evidently so were her parents as they shared a moment of eye contact that Ashlee could only call shock. Her father raised his brown eyebrows in amazement.

Her mother cleared her throat. "Okay. Rex and Tristan can fill in what I don't know. We should all be able to hear one another. Your father is my mate, we've been through the mating ritual, and that makes him pack. He'll hear Tristan, as well. You can hear Tristan because you're his mate, even though you haven't yet done the ritual." She paused to take a breath then gestured to Tristan's brother. "Now, you won't be able to hear Rex if he goes into telepathy until you go through the ritual and officially become pack, so Rex, keep the talking to the spoken kind for Ashlee's sake."

Rex nodded.

Ashlee stared at her mother and wondered if she'd ever really seen her before. Always the prettiest woman in the room, to Ashlee and her sister she was ethereal, untouchable. But now, Ashlee could see that beyond Victoria's blonde hair and blue-eyed appearance, stood a woman who possessed a will of steel. She had attacked the Snake man with no hesitation even though she was the smallest wolf in the group.

Had there been any sign of any of this when she'd been growing up? Her mother had been strong and confident. She'd never gotten caught up in any of the pettiness that some of her friend's mothers had seemed preoccupied with. Often they would catch her staring out in the distance, lost in thought. She'd pushed her father professionally and he'd thrived under her influence. Ashlee had been less motivated by her mother's involvement, always feeling like she didn't quite measure up or that she was being judged somehow to see if she was different

But this level of odd Ashlee never could have foreseen.

"You see darling, we are wolf-shifters." Ashlee opened her mouth to ask a question but her mother cut her off by raising her left index finger. "Or in simple terms, we can take the form of a wolf when we want to. In fact, some of us prefer to live as animals. But not me, I've always felt more human. It's not clear why we can do it, but people from our families have had this ability for at least five hundred years or more. Some people think it's magic. Some of our kind can even do magic. Before I left the island, I had learned a few simple spells I could control pretty well. I've seen enough to believe our shifts are mystical in their origin. Unlike others, I don't need another reason for what I can do." She blew out a breath and sat in silence.

Our kind?

What did that mean?

They weren't human. Her mother had said she'd hoped Ashlee was just a human girl. What was she if not human? She pinched the inside of her arm, she certainly felt human. She didn't know what to say so she simply said nothing at all, her heart pounding in her chest.

Tristan crossed the room to sit at her feet. *Ashlee, don't you have any questions about this?*

"I saw what happened tonight. I know you all

became wolves." She swallowed. "Is Dad a wolf too?"

Her father shook his head. "No baby, I'm not a wolf. Just an ordinary human."

Ashlee nodded. "Like me. I've never become a wolf."

Her mother rose. "No, honey. We don't know if you can become a wolf or not. I never saw any sign of it in you but the truth is that really doesn't mean anything. Your first change, the first time you shift into wolf form, should be with a pack. Significant magic must be present to facilitate the first change. I went out of my way to never use magic around you but my little bit of mystical abilities would not have been enough even if I had to push a change on you."

Ashlee shook her head. "Why do you have to be with the pack?"

"Well you don't have to be. But it's dangerous if you're not. If a lone wolf awakened by itself, it could be detrimental. The wolf needs to feel the Pack immediately to know it's not alone in the world. Sometimes the second and third shift too, but my family has always been strong and the wolf and person are usually fine after the first time. Also, it usually takes a combined effort of the whole pack and the influence of the Alpha to bring on enough magic." Her mother wrung her hands. "I've kept you from the pack. So, we don't know if you can do it or not. Even if you can't shift, you're still obviously unique—what we call latent. You would still have some paranormal gifts that regular humans don't have."

"So you knew I might be, what is the word—latent—and you still said nothing?"

Her mother nodded and Ashlee bit her tongue. They'd been through this already but it still ate at her gut.

Tristan raised his head for a moment. *She had a prophetic dream tonight. That's why she came to the zoo.*

Her mother sucked in her breath and gripped Ashlee's arm. "Does this happen all the time? Or is it just the time with that horrible vision and now this one?"

Ashlee suddenly felt incredibly uncomfortable that everyone in the room stared at her. She stood up. "No. I think this was just these two times."

Her mother looked down at the floor and her father shook his head. "You always had very bad dreams as a child, so intense, so real to you. The pediatrician told us it was normal, that you just had an active imagination. We should have known better. Again, your mother and I have become the king and queen of self-delusion."

Rex snorted. "That's for damn sure."

Enough Rex.

Ashlee was glad Tristan said something. It was one thing for her to be annoyed at her family, it was another for someone else to butt in.

"About thirty years ago, darling, our pack leader—Tristan and Rex's father—came to know a man named Claudius Brouseax. Our pack had lived quietly and without problems for one hundred years on an island off the coast of Maine called Westervelt. You won't find it on any map. It's very small, about fifteen square miles, most of it forest. I assume that is still the case?" Her mother looked at Tristan and Rex and they both nodded. "Kendrick was our pack leader and we trusted him implicitly."

Tristan jumped up on the couch and put his head on Ashlee's lap. Rex paced at the window and then turned around before he spoke. "Claudius convinced my father, or maybe my father convinced Claudius, that there was money to be made off shifters. We are human and animal. We think and reason like humans and possess the loyalty and instincts of wolves. Both live within us and it is a constant battle for control, but a glorious one. We live very long lives. Until we are thirty we age as a human does, and then we stop, and do not age again until we mate."

"You guys don't age until you have sex?" Ashlee's mind whirled. Only Tristan's head in her lap kept her seated.

No, little one, by mate he means bond. It is much like love but more-so. It is eternal, the way all love should be but is not always. Ours really is forever, it cannot be destroyed once it is found. We recognize in the other person the other half of our own soul and we remain together until death.

"What happens when you die?" Tristan's wolf eyes narrowed at the question and Ashlee swallowed hard.

Usually when one dies, the other does too.

Ashlee tried to speak but her voice came out a whisper. "That's horrible."

Her mother answered instead of Tristan. "It's beautiful…I would never want to live a second without your father, not a millisecond."

Ashlee watched Tristan do the equivalent of a wolf-shrug.

The remaining spouse is overwhelmed with a desire to follow their other half to the next life.

Ashlee couldn't believe what she heard. Did the remaining spouse just drop dead? "How does that work?"

They commit, what we call, ritual suicide. Unless there is a child to raise, in which case the parent waits to die until the child is old enough. Then, they too, are overwhelmed with the need to leave. We simply cannot live without the other. And those who try to resist the urge, are doomed to living forever in agony…most do not try to resist.

Ashlee's head spun and she shivered. "What happens if you don't find your mate? Do you stay thirty eternally?"

Unless we commit suicide, yes, or are killed.

Suicide?

Her mother paced the room. "So, honey, I began aging when I met your father. Until then I'd been thirty for about seventy-five years. Rex here, although he looks thirty, is three years my senior. I don't know how old Tristan is. You were with the pack when they came to Maine one hundred years ago, yes?

That's right. I was one year old. Tristan's wolf eyes bore into Ashlee's. Was he waiting for her to freak out?

Another couple of minutes and she might oblige if she didn't have a panic attack before then. Once again, she wiped her sweaty hands on her pants. *I am the third of six boys. My two older brothers are so old they've stopped counting.*

"How did you even meet Dad, Mom? Why aren't you on the island with all of them?" She gestured towards Rex and Tristan.

"Thirty years ago, everyone went crazy." Her mother swallowed. Rex slammed his back into the wall which shook the pastoral watercolor that hung there so violently it almost fell off the wall. Rex's hand steadied it before it did. Her mother continued, "Our pack leader brought Claudius to the island. It seemed strange. The only non-wolves on the island were mates of shifters. He was not. Claudius wanted to take the essence of the wolves in us and find a way to inject it into regular humans. He thought he could create an army of super-strong, aggressive, animal-like humans who would serve him. Kendrick wanted us to let him experiment on us. We objected. If I recall correctly, Trip here was the most ardent against the procedures." Tristan growled and Ashlee stroked his head again. He settled down and closed his eyes.

"I was still mateless. In the middle of the night, our Alpha's wife, Mary Jo, Tristan and Rex's mother, awakened me. Part of what makes the Royals so special, so unique among us, is that something in their bloodline is different. An Alpha and his mate can live forever until he steps down or dies. Mary Jo looked twenty years old but she'd been alive for centuries. She told us that her mate had lost his mind. He'd brought in a witch…"

Ashlee jerked in her chair. "A witch?" Shape-shifters she could accept, she had no choice as she'd seen it herself, but witches?

You've been listening to this whole story and the witch is what you object to? Ashlee thought she heard a laugh in Tristan's voice.

Rex stepped forward. "Kendrick, our father, had brought in a witch. He was going to kill all the unmated females, including babies and children, and then use the witch to cast a spell that would get our men to kill their mates if we didn't consent to the testing. He'd gone to fetch the witch from the mainland. Our mother was an extraordinary woman. It takes a lot to defy your mate, especially if he is the Alpha of your pack. But she did. She grabbed all of the unmated women and sent them off all over the world. When the men awoke, we did not know what had happened to them. Our mother was an extraordinary mystic in her own right. She masked them with her magic so we could not find them. However, the mated women refused to leave."

Ashlee swallowed hard. "And did their mates kill them?"

Yes. They were completely changed by the spell; they could not control themselves or stop the need to kill their mates. All but two, that is. My uncles, my father's brothers, did not harm their women. They took their own lives instead. My Aunts remain alive to this day in agony, but as the only women still present in our pack—and only women can be healers—they must remain with us until some women return who can take over the mystical positions. Every day for the last thirty years has been a struggle for my Aunts... every minute that they are alive they are wishing for death to rejoin their mates.

"They still live then, all these years, they exist with the pain?" Ashlee's mother's eyes filled up with tears and Ashlee had to swallow her shock. Her mother never cried and this was twice in ten minutes she'd almost lost it.

"Our father killed our mother before the spell was even finished. He is also not dead. It seems he has found a way to circumvent the kill-yourself-when-your-mate-dies impulse." Rex snorted. "The other men, when they realized what happened, what they had done to the most precious thing in the world to them, their mates, they killed themselves immediately. It was gruesome and awful." Rex paused in his speech, his eyes deep and fathomless. Ashlee wondered if he was reliving that time. She was grateful to not have those memories herself.

"My father thought he could control us with the threat of killing our future mates, but they were already gone, sent away by our mother. He killed her before he knew this, so she couldn't tell him where they were. Trip and Theo, our fifth brother, the one right above me in age, led the attack on our father but he got away.

"Our mother had made the spell so that only when the danger had passed could we locate our missing women. That's why the spell has never lifted and we have not been able to find anyone. Thirty men live on that island waiting the return of our missing girls—or at least the ability to find them, to know if they still live. Our eldest brother Michael has been acting as interim Alpha ever since. But he has no taste for the job. And obviously the danger is not over as Father's men attempted to get Tristan six months ago. We feared him dead. But evidently he'd just been trapped as a wolf and living in a zoo."

After they stunned me with their magic while I waited for you, I managed to limp off into the woods. When I woke up I was in the back of an animal control truck on my way to New Jersey with no way to shift back. Whatever they did to me with their magic, they trapped me in this form and it's been agony. Why have none of you ever tried to come home, Victoria?

"Mary Jo told us to go live our lives as humans. She said our magic would keep us safe as long as we were not together. So we split up, the little girls sent to orphanages and homes. I don't know where they are. I thought to wait until the danger was over and I could come home." Victoria turned to Ashlee, she had a small smile on her face.

"I was so lost at first. Live as a human? What did that mean? We'd been raised to fear exposure, to stay away from spending too much time out amongst non-shifters. Kendrick could barely stand the shifters whose mates were humans. Mary Jo sent me to New York City. It was horrible at first. Where were the places to run as a wolf? There was so much noise, so many people. I worked odd jobs. I waitressed but I broke everything I touched and I couldn't keep orders straight. Finally, a woman I met on the subway who took pity on me got me a job at Columbia Presbyterian in the cafeteria. I sliced off the top half of my finger and that's how I met Scott. And the wolf wants what it wants. My mate was human. Kendrick would hate me and I could care less." Ashlee's mom looked up and smiled at her. "I had you and your sister and I did not need to go back. I made myself forget."

Ashlee had heard that story before. But they'd said her mother had been a student earning extra cash at the hospital. This version was very different.

Rex's head jerked up. "Sister?"

Her mother's eyes flared and Ashlee knew that whatever she was about to say would be her mother's final word on the subject. Twenty-two years had taught Ashlee to be careful of her mother's stubborn streak. "She is in college and I will not give her to the Pack until she is at least Ashlee's age, and then only if she has a mate, as Ashlee does. I won't have her passed around the group of you just because you're lonesome for female companionship."

Ashlee took a deep breath and cut off Rex's response. She stared straight at Tristan, the word she uttered being of the upmost importance. "I can't be your mate, Tristan. I can't have any children. You'll want to find someone else."

Her father looked sad. "The doctors have told us

that Ashlee's reproductive organs, her ovaries and her uterus, simply do not work. Pregnancy is impossible without ovulation and the doctors aren't sure her uterus could support a pregnancy even with someone else's egg. It's malformed." Ashlee groaned. She hated when her father talked about what was such a personal, terrible fact of her life as if it was simply another medical discussion.

Tears stung the back of Ashlee's eyes but she did not shed them. She'd gone down this road before. Tom had been so sure his family would never accept him marrying a barren woman he'd gone and cheated on her with some girl who worked at the dairy queen, and the ultimate irony of the whole thing was that he had knocked her up. Ashlee didn't even know Tristan. Losing him couldn't possibly be as great a loss as losing Tom over her infertility.

I don't care.

"You don't care?" Ashlee and her mother spat out at the same time.

No.

Her mother narrowed her eyes at Tristan. "You male shifters are all about the mating and the babies. How can you not care?"

Tristan made a snorting noise and opened his eyes. *I could make generalities about female shifters, would you like that, Victoria?*

Her mother shook her head and said nothing else.

Rex advanced on her mother, his hand on hips. "You should have brought your daughters to us the second they were born. They should have been raised on our island. With the pack."

Her father, always the peacemaker, spoke softly. "We considered it. But Vicki was worried since you didn't seek her out, the danger might not be gone, which evidently it isn't, and also, Ashlee attached so early on to Tom, we thought he must be her mate."

Who is Tom?

Ashlee pushed Tristan gently off her lap and stood. She walked to the other side of the room. "It doesn't matter. He's gone now. He married someone else. I don't know about this mate thing." She still needed to clarify some things in her own mind. She turned to her mother. "There was nothing about me as a child that led you to believe I could be like you?"

Her mother shook her head. "Other than the dreams that your father just reminded me of, no there was not. Don't forget Ashlee, I had no one to guide me in raising a half-shifter. I had no idea what to look for or how to tell. You were an imaginative, smart, wonderful little girl. But when you didn't start to rage around puberty, when you didn't start to demand release from our parental bounds, I didn't think you had the wolf in you."

Ashlee sucked in her breath. A sudden thought occurred to her. "But Summer raged. She still does. She defies you at every turn." Her mother nodded slowly. "Oh, I see, you thought I was normal but you didn't believe Summer was."

"And that's why we've had to be so hard on her, so

controlling of where she goes and who she knows. I know she's got the wolf. But I won't let it come out, not until she's mature enough to protect herself."

It all started to make sense to Ashlee. She needed to say something and she wasn't sure she could. She swallowed and clenched her fists at her side. "You've never understood my nature." Ashlee's voice wavered and she forced herself to pull it together. She pointed at her father. "But you should have."

Her father looked down and her mother put her hands on her hips. "What do you mean Ash?"

Ashlee placed her hands over her heart. "I rage here." Her voice came out a whisper but she knew enough now to know that with their wolf hearing they all heard what she said. She wasn't finished. Tristan needed an answer from her. "I've just met you and I don't even know what you look like as a human." *Except in my dreams*, she added silently.

All of this we will work out when we get back home. Rex, call Michael. I cannot. Rex nodded and followed Ashlee's father from the room.

Her mother turned around, her expression stricken. "Ash, do you want to go to Maine with Trip and Rex?"

Ashlee said nothing for a moment. Did she? This could be a chance to start again. Hadn't she just been thinking that morning, that it was time to move forward? Her hands tingled. "If all of this is true, then I think I should go see it for myself, don't you? But I want your promise Tristan, that I can leave anytime I want." Her mother smiled proudly at her request.

His eyes turned gentle when he looked at Ashlee. *Anytime. I would not hold you against your will. Ever.*

She sighed in relief.

"Trip, I implore you, she has been raised entirely as a human. That's my fault, my decision. She knows nothing of our ways. Please treat her kindly. Her wolf must be very strong if its forcing visions on her without her ever having shifted. Perhaps I should come with her."

Victoria, we revere our mates. Have you been gone so long you cannot remember? We will work out Ashlee's shift when we get to Westervelt. You are welcome to come; it is your home, always.

Ashlee's father shook his head. "No." Her mother looked up shocked. "If Ashlee does this thing, it's her experience to have. We've hidden her from herself. We'll not interfere in her mating."

Victoria's voice shook but she held her stance. "I had other reasons for keeping her from the pack and not letting her come into contact with magic. I would not have her mated to a man who can be bewitched to kill her." Her mother held her head high but fear simmered in her eyes. Ashlee's eyes widened. These people were royalty to her mother and yet she stood up to them.

I would kill myself before that happened.

"You would doom both of you to death, then?"

She could choose to follow or not like my Aunts did.

"And condemn her to a torturous existence?" Her mother advanced on the wolf. "You are your father's son, how can you be so sure of what you would do?" Silence filled the room, the kind that usually precipitated one of her mother's explosion, but Tristan lay down, his head on the floor.

I am my mother's son.

"Let's hope so, shall we?"

****

Tristan watched Ashlee go upstairs to pack a bag. Her mother had told her to pack enough clothes for a week. She would be gone much longer than a week, if Tristan had anything to say about it. She was his mate, it was true, but the problems that both Ashlee and Victoria had brought up were legitimate.

What if she didn't think he was handsome?

What if she wanted to leave to lead a life away from the pack? That one was easy. He would leave with her. If Vicki could live off-island as a human for decades, so could he, once he was turned back to his human form. He would gladly go wherever Ashlee wanted.

But Vicki's greatest charge still rang in his ears. Was he his father's son? Could a witch wielding dark magic force him to harm his beloved? No. His uncles had resisted. So could he.

He hoped.

Chapter Three

Rex was loaded up on painkillers and out cold in the backseat of her mother's minivan. She had insisted they use the van because it had better safety features than Ashlee's SUV. She'd shoved the keys in Ashlee's hand before quietly whispering that she shouldn't worry about finding Tristan handsome, Trip had always been a 'babe.'

Ashlee had grimaced at that remark. It was gross that her mother had once been in a position to notice whether or not Tristan was handsome in that way. But truthfully, it wasn't the weirdest part of the whole situation so she might as well let it go.

Tristan lay across the front seat, eyes closed, panting heavily.

She'd been driving for four hours and was about to enter the Boston area. Her eyes felt heavy, they drooped as she concentrated on not letting them shut. Her parents had wanted them to stay the night at their house but the idea of poor Tristan having to spend any more time than necessary stuck as a wolf seemed cruel to her. Now she wished she'd taken them up on their offer. She needed to pull over to sleep or find a hotel. But what kind of hotel could she bring a wolf and a drugged up injured man into at six in the morning? Her lids fluttered. She jerked them open and turned up the air conditioner. Even with the cold air hitting her in the face at full blast, she could barely keep her eyes open.

What's the matter, little one?

Ashlee jumped an inch in her seat and laughed. She looked down at Tristan, his eyes wide. She'd thought he was asleep.

"I'm falling asleep at the wheel. We need to stop."

I'm so tired of being trapped like this. I should be driving. You should rest. You've been through an ordeal.

She shook her head. "I think you've been through more of an ordeal than me."

Rex, wake up!

Rex leaped in his seat, eyes wide. "What is it, big brother?" He rubbed his eyes.

Is your head clear?

"It can't possibly be, Tristan. My Dad gave him a whole bunch of pills."

We absorb painkillers differently than humans. My brother should be more than able to handle the wheel. Look--there's a truck stop at the next exit and we can stop.

"I'll drive." Rex nodded. Ashlee pulled the car into the truck stop and let Rex get in the front. She climbed into the backseat and Tristan climbed over the center console to be with her.

"Is Rex your real name?" Seemed a little funny that his name was Rex when he spent time as a canine. Ashlee remembered reading kid stories where the dog was almost always named Rex.

"No. Randolph Kane, at your service." He gave her a mock salute in the rearview mirror. She laughed and Tristan growled.

"His jealousy will subside after you perform the mating ritual. Then you'll be able to speak to other males and not worry that his head is going to spin off."

A warm fuzzy feeling spread through Ashlee. She'd never had anyone act jealous about her before.

Sleep. Tristan lay across the floor in front of her.

Now that she wasn't driving, she felt wired, her heart pounded in her chest and she couldn't settle down. "I don't think I can."

You can. Shut your eyes, my Ashlee. You'll be out in minutes.

"You're creative with the endearments." But she obliged him by closing her eyes.

Ashlee?

She opened her eyes. "I told you I wouldn't be able to sleep."

We've arrived at the ferry. You've been asleep for five hours, little one. He made a snort that had to be the wolf version of a laugh. Ashlee sat up and stretched her neck. Her muscles felt stiff. She must have slept in the same position for the whole five hours.

"I'm sorry I fell asleep for so long, Rex."

He shrugged. "I like driving. This thing actually gets great gas mileage."

Ashlee peered out the window at her surroundings. They were parked at a boat dock, although no boat was in sight. An old decrepit wooden shack stood to the left of the dock. She opened her door and stepped out. "Ooh." She shivered and rubbed her arms. It was much colder in Maine than in New Jersey. The colors of the leaves varied from a deep brown and red to gold, even purple, a strange occurrence for so early in the season, especially since back at home they were still green.

The wind chased about her and she shivered again. Rex walked up next to her and leaned on the van. He wore her father's black sweatpants and grey sweatshirt, which were small on him as if his clothes had shrunk in the dryer.

Tristan rubbed against her legs and she looked down at him. She patted his head absentmindedly and he closed his eyes under her touch. She smiled.

Her Wolf

"Does it feel good to be almost home?"

I will feel better when we get off the boat and onto our land. Rex, go get the cage. I hear the boat.

Rex nodded and walked to the back of the boathouse. He emerged with a metal cage that he quickly opened.

Ashlee's heart thumped in her chest. "Why do you have to be caged?"

The man who runs the ferry doesn't know who we are. He thinks this is a wolf preserve and that we run it. He would be very unhappy with a wolf running loose on his boat.

"Oh." She really hated the idea of Tristan caged. But he didn't seem to mind. He walked into the metal cage and Rex snapped the door shut.

"Lucky us, Ashlee." He winked. "Only way to keep him contained." Tristan growled. "I joke, big brother, that's all."

Ashlee shivered again but this time not from the cold. Hadn't Tristan thought Rex betrayed him? What did she really know of Rex, anyway? Not that she knew Tristan either. Ashlee's pulse sped up and her stomach twisted. Why had she thought it was a good idea to come to this place?

The boat flowed smoothly in the water alongside the dock. It looked like a small fishing vessel, the kind she'd seen in Martha's Vineyard when they'd vacationed there a decade ago. It didn't seem like a ferry. Wooden and old, it let out a puff of black smoke when it came to a complete stop.

"Don't worry, it'll float. And don't talk to Trip on the way over there. The seaman will think you're nuts. We have to replace them every five years as it is so they don't notice that we don't age." Rex whispered.

"Why don't some of you just learn to drive a boat? You could send one of those telepathic messages across the water: 'send speed boat now.'" Ashlee looked at the rough dark water they were about to cross. Not that she wanted to pilot the boat. She wasn't volunteering or anything.

Rex shrugged. "We have a lot of things we need to update around here, customs, like the ferry-man, which haven't been changed in way too long. One of us should become a boat captain, but the telepathy thing, it doesn't work over long distances like that."

Ashlee nodded. "Oh." What else needed to be updated? Were they living in huts with no indoor plumbing? Ashlee swallowed, her mouth dry.

"Got a wolf you're bringing over, Mister Kane?" The old sailor seemed straight out of a movie. He wore a patch over his left eye. His hair, completely white, thinned in the back. He wore a black rain slicker and overalls.

"I do, Peter. Not to worry, he's properly caged. Plus this one's been castrated. He's not going to harm anyone." Ashlee heard Tristan give a low growl in the cage. She wanted desperately to reach through the cage bars and touch him. But, you didn't do that to regular wolves, and it wouldn't do to make the captain suspicious. "This is Ashlee Morrison. She's joining us at

Her Wolf

the Institute."

"Welcome." Peter extended his hand and she shook it. "Where is your coat?"

"Packed." She hoped she remembered to pack her coat.

"Why don't you go below where it's warmer?"

"Thanks, but I'll be fine." She wasn't leaving Tristan and Rex. She stood by the railing and looked out at the water as the boat slowly plowed over the sea. The water was choppy. In general, she didn't get seasick but this ride pushed even her limits. The boat rocked right and shook left as the vessel groaned beneath them. Ashlee scanned the deck for life preservers and didn't see any.

She stared out in the distance and watched as the island got closer. There it was: Wolf Island, they had called it Westervelt, where wolf-shifters had lived for a century unbothered by mankind. The place her mother had fled in the middle of the night in a run for her life. Visions of a young woman, huddled over, hidden, terrified, knowing that she might never come home again filled Ashlee's mind.

One lone tear slipped from the vision of young Victoria's eye and Ashlee sucked in her breath. It seemed so real what she'd imagined. Ashlee wanted to reach out and grab the young woman and assure her that a young man doing his Emergency Room rotation—her mate—waited in New York City to sew up the top of her finger after she cut it off at the cafeteria job she worked. But the vision waned and Ashlee was brought back to her current situation.

She focused on the land mass as it grew closer. Westervelt wasn't too big and most of the island appeared to be wooded. Big, thick, dense trees filled with color like on the mainland. She didn't see any housing. They did sleep indoors didn't they? Her heart pounded in her chest. Rex seemed content not to speak which left her alone with her thoughts. Ashlee didn't know if this was a good thing or not. Finally, after what felt like forever, they docked on the island.

Rex crossed the deck to retrieve Tristan's cage. Ashlee started to walk forward when Peter grabbed her arm. He tugged her to his side. She pulled back from his hold but his fingernails dug into her skin. She cried out.

"Turn back. I'll take you back right now. Things are not right over there. Satan lives on that island. The animals, they're not right. These people do weird work with the wolves. I'll take you back, miss. Come with me now."

Ashlee stared at him with her mouth open to speak but Rex was suddenly behind her. "Peter, what do you think you're doing to Ms. Morrison?"

Ashlee finally managed to free herself from the old man's grip and she almost fell backward from the effort. When she turned around, she had to stifle a whimper. A growl erupted from the metal cage but that wasn't what frightened her. Rex's eyes had gone dark, menacing. They were his wolf eyes. Ashlee worried that in one moment Rex would shift and then Peter's days were finished.

Her Wolf

"Thank you for your concern, sir. I'll be fine." She tried to smile as she crossed past Rex and the cage, and then hopefully to the boat exit. She looked down as she walked; glad she was on solid ground. When Rex had finally taken the cage off the boat and joined her, she whirled to look at him.

"I thought you were going to shift right there."

"I had it under control. But I would have shifted if he didn't let you go. We obviously need to get a new ferryboat operator. He threatened the pack."

He was right, little one. We do not let others harm those who belong to us.

Tristan didn't need to say more. The unspoken words lay out before them like a bridge she need only cross. If she was pack, she belonged to them, as she belonged to Tristan. She swallowed hard. Did she really want to be owned like that? Once the boat was far enough away, Rex opened up the cage, Tristan walked out. He stretched as he pushed his front paws down towards the ground.

Ashlee didn't move an inch as she said, "I don't belong to anyone. You told me I could leave when I wanted to, Tristan."

You can. But even if you run to the ends of the earth, you will still belong to our pack. You are one of us.

That sounded like a big problem. She never got the chance to respond as four wolves ran out from behind the trees. The biggest one held a bag in his mouth that he dropped on the ground in front of him. She guessed they weren't just regular wolves. Seemed a pretty solid bet they were shifters come to greet them.

A band of white light suddenly engulfed the four wolves. Ashlee covered her eyes with her hands as it momentarily blinded her. When it cleared, the wolves' bones snapped and pulled as they grew larger in front of her eyes. She gasped. She'd never actually seen anyone shift before. Moreover, she could feel their magic in her own bones. Her stomach stirred. She put her hand on her belly to stop the grumble. She wasn't hungry; it was more like pain shot through her intestines and her stomach didn't know how to deal with it.

The shift finished, and four men of various heights—all of them tall and naked—stood in front of her. Rex crossed to the tallest and hugged him awkwardly. They embraced for a moment before the four naked men opened the bag they had dragged and quickly clothed themselves.

As they dressed, the tallest in the group spoke. "Greetings Rex. I see you found our brother. Locked in a zoo, was he?" The man who spoke had to be six foot five or taller. He had blond hair and brown eyes, the same as Rex's. Was that what Tristan's eyes looked like when he wasn't a wolf?

Locked in a zoo. Yes. Snicker if you must.

"We must," the tall brother remarked again and the other three cracked up laughing. She looked at him. Each one had varying degrees of brownish-blonde hair, cut short. The darkest of the group was also the smallest. Now that she could see five of Tristan's brothers together, she could make out the family resemblance between them. The Kane brothers all possessed the same high cheekbones. Identical noses protruded proudly from their face. It was the jaw line and the eyes that differentiated them.

"This must be your mate. " The tall one who Rex embraced stepped forward. "The whole island awaits you with great anticipation. We think very highly of your mother. I'm Michael Kane."

Our Alpha.

"Just for now." Michael amended Tristan. "And this is Gabriel." He pointed to the man who stood to his left. Gabriel stepped forward and bowed. Ashlee swallowed, unsure of what to do. How did one answer such a gesture? Gabriel was only slightly smaller than Michael. His jaw line was round, where Michael's had been long. Also, he had a cleft in his chin, and his bangs were unevenly cut.

Rex rolled his eyes at Gabriel. "Don't mind Gabriel, he doesn't leave the island much. He doesn't know that we don't bow to women anymore." Gabriel looked stricken and took a step back.

"Its—ah—nice to meet you and thank you for bowing, that was a very nice way to be welcomed," she hurried to add at his obvious discomfort. His eyes looked at her kindly.

"And this one over here who is younger than Trip by one year is Theo. Don't be grumpy--come say hello to Trip's mate."

Ashlee had to force herself to stay still when Theo stepped forward. His eyes were huge and brown; he clenched his jaw so tightly that Ashlee could see the muscles strain. Did he already dislike her?

"You look like your mother." He extended his hand and she took it. His voice sounded cold. Maybe it was her mother he didn't like? She thought he would shake her hand but he brought it to his lips and kissed it. Tristan growled. Theo raised his head to look at Tristan. "Just checking."

Just checking what?

"And finally we have the one who is just one year older than Rex here and that is Azriel. "

Azriel's chin was very similar to Michael's but no one would mix them up. He was the smallest of the group. He also had the broadest shoulders. One long thin line scarred his face from his left eye to his neck. He shook her hand cheerfully and she smiled.

She needed to say something. "Your Mom liked very strong names."

For some reason, this struck all six of them as funny and they all burst out laughing hysterically. She tried to smile. Even Tristan snorted through his nose.

"She did." Michael smiled. "Welcome home."

Home? Could she ever think of this as home? She doubted it. Her parents' white stucco house seemed more and more appealing. She glanced over her shoulder. Maybe she could make a run for it. All she had to was swim the four miles across the river. Mmm, maybe not.

Michael looked down at Tristan with seriousness. "We need to get your problem taken care of immediately, Trip, so we can go about figuring out how this happened, how we can ward for it, and who betrayed us. I must tell you, some started to fear you were dead."

Some?

Michael grinned. "Okay, me. "

Let me get Ashlee settled and then I would love for all of you to turn me back.

Theo grinned then. "Count on it, my brother, count on it."

Ashlee stood in the middle of Tristan's room. She walked from wall to wall as she admired the artwork. They had that in common. If she couldn't find anything else to say to him at least they could discuss painting. 'Getting Ashlee settled' had turned out to mean depositing her in his bedroom and asking her if she would be okay for a few hours on her own. She'd nodded and he'd turned to leave, before he came back with a strange warning.

Don't worry if you hear odd things tonight. They're going to be forcing a lot of magic onto me to turn me back. Don't be afraid, little one.

Then he'd run out again. She appreciated that Tristan had taken the time to warn her.

Now she could obsess about what they were doing out there tonight. She heard a howl out in the distant night and walked to the window. Nothing but trees and darkness. And thirty male shifters who hadn't seen a female of their kind for thirty years. She shivered at the thought. She walked to the door and locked it. Not that it would keep anyone out who really wanted to get in, but it made her feel moderately safer. Tristan couldn't be too much longer…she'd just get up and let him in when he knocked.

The room felt colder than before and she opened her suitcase to rummage for a sweater. Undecided on whether she'd stay or not, she hadn't put anything away. There was nowhere to put her things had she wanted to. Tristan obviously hadn't been expecting a roommate when he'd last left the place. No empty hangers in the closet, no room in any drawers.

Most surprising was the big screen television that faced the bed. She'd expected everything to be rustic, but inside the house was modern and updated. She turned on the television. Did they get any reception here or did they just watch DVDs?

Ashlee changed the channel and sighed in relief when she found a full array of satellite television channels presented to her. So, there were some modern conveniences in this strange place. Another howl in the night ruined her mood for late-night Jay Leno and she turned off the television. She walked to the window and looked out. Was that Tristan out there howling? Goosebumps rose on her arms and she tried to massage them away with her hands. In her entire life, she'd never felt so alone.

She crossed to the chair next to the bed and sat down. She rubbed her eyes and yawned. When Tristan

Her Wolf

got back, she would tell him—whether he was a wolf or a man—to take her home. She closed her eyes to rest them for a moment. Just for a moment...

Ashlee jerked awake and fell out of the chair. She closed her eyes to avoid the sheer torture that had awoken her. She rolled onto the floor and screamed out in pain and agony. Every bone in her body felt like it had just broken. She tried to use her legs and couldn't. She opened her eyes and looked down at her hands. They shook of their own volition and fur rapidly spread over her skin. She screamed out again but no one answered. How long had she been asleep? Where was Tristan? Who was doing this to her? Her mother had said she needed to be with the pack to change. Something bad would happen to her wolf if she was alone.

Were they making this happen?

Was Tristan torturing her for not being sure she could be his mate? He'd known this could happen. Yet he left her.

She sucked in her breath and gave one last yell that sounded like a stifled yelp. She rolled over onto her stomach and stood up on all fours. She looked around. Everything felt different. The clothes she'd worn were ripped into shreds and spread out on the floor around her. Her skin was covered in white and red fur.

I'm a wolf.

Her head shot upwards. Everything felt incredibly clear. She could smell scents in the room that she'd never noticed before. Tristan. He was everywhere, and he smelled like nighttime and pine trees. Why hadn't she noticed? Her eyes darted from side to side and she pushed her head down to the floor.

Alone. I am so alone. I have no family. I'm not meant to be alone. I have no pack to love me.

She howled in agony, this time not from physical pain, but loneliness. She needed to get out of this room. It did not belong to her. She did not know these people and they did not love her. They had left her to hurt all by herself. She ran for the door but could not wedge it open with her paw and her snout. No luck. It would not open.

Out. Need to get out.

Only one other way out of the room. She stared out the window and looked down. Not too far. Two stories. She could make it if she broke through the window. She leapt at it and it gave under her weight. As the glass shattered around her, it cut at her front paws and sides. She howled again as her momentum took her out the window. She hit the ground with a thump and her paws burned. She walked for a moment despite the limp she'd just given herself.

I'm free and I am all alone. Forever.

She ran for the woods in front of her. Every step she took was agony. If she was to be alone, this would be the best place to lose herself.

Chapter Four

Tristan walked towards the main house, or the Institute as the outside world thought of it, and shook his limbs. His brothers followed close behind him, but none of them were in as big a hurry to get back as he was.

It felt awesome to be back in his human body. His limbs felt so loose. Michael droned about plans to finally find their father, but Tristan wasn't listening. His whole mind was intent on getting back to Ashlee. The pack had taken much longer than he'd expected to bring him out of his wolf body. Eight hours of magic and it had hurt like hell the whole time.

He pulled his tee-shirt over his head, his pants already on, and once again thanked the fates that Theo had thought to bring along a change of clothes for him. Tristan needed to court Ashlee and coming to her completely naked would not be a great way to start. She'd been raised as a human. She wasn't going to just accept him because his wolf claimed her. He smiled as he pictured her wandering around his room. What had she thought of his artwork?

"Trip?" Theo clipped and Tristan turned around to see what had happened.

Tristan didn't see anything amiss. "What?"

"Look." Theo pointed at the second floor of the house and Tristan's gaze followed his finger to the shattered window of Tristan's bedroom Glass littered the grass below. His heart fell into his stomach

"Ashlee!" He ran, faster than he ever had on human legs, into the house. Theo was right behind him and he knew the others would be too. He turned the corner down the long hallway that led to his room, his pulse pounding hard in his ears. The wolf wanted back and tried to force himself into his eyes as the dryness that precipitated the shift from man to wolf started inside of him.

He grabbed the door handle. It was locked. What the hell? He banged on the door. "Ashlee?"

No answer. He shoved his weight against it.

"Wait." Theo called as he caught up. "I have keys to all the rooms." Tristan watched as Theo fumbled with the keys in his hands.

Tristan paced in front of the door. "Come on. Come on."

"Got it." Theo barely unlocked the door when it swung open. Tristan thrust his brother aside to get into the room. Empty. His eyes scanned the scene. Glass by the window. Her clothes, ripped, on the floor. Oh God, no.

"Dad?" He spun to Theo, Mike, and Rex who had joined him inside the room. "Did Dad take her?"

"Calm down. " Mike placed his hand on his shoulder. "Take a deep breath. This is wolf, but not Dad, and not one whose scent I recognize."

Tristan forced himself to focus. Going off half-crazed would not help find Ashlee. He closed his eyes and inhaled deeply. Mike was right. Wolf. Ashlee had been here. He could smell everywhere she'd gone in the room. He picked up the shreds of her clothes and sniffed. Wolf. There was wolf on her clothes.

Realization staggered Tristan. He took one more deep breath at the fabric in his hands. She'd shifted. Ashlee was the wolf. The magic they'd thrown on him last night had been strong and powerful. Somehow that much magic had made its way to Ashlee and forced her shift. Tristan could feel his blood pressure rise. She'd been alone.

"Not good." Mike whispered. "She's shifted all by herself. How could that even happen? It shouldn't have been able to happen without the pack magic. She's alone."

Theo nodded and desperation twisted Tristan's gut. "You can lose yourself in your wolf the first time if you're all alone." Tristan was more than aware of this fact.

Tristan swallowed hard. He rushed to the window then stuck his head out and inhaled. "She's got to be terrified but she went into the woods."

"She won't know how to hunt." Theo stood beside Tristan, Mike on the other side.

Michael nodded. "Some things are instinctual, but we need to get her back. She needs to bond with the pack, become a member, and respond to us. But she barely knows me. I'm not her Alpha yet. Tristan you're going to have to go and get her. You're her mate. She'll recognize you, whether she realizes it or not."

Damn it, he'd failed her already. He should have been there, been by her side as she made the change for the first time. Goddamn it. What if he lost her? He'd just found her. But the possibility of losing her to the wolf forever was grave.

He turned to his brother. "There is still enough time to save her. There has to be."

Michael nodded. "You have to hurry, Tristan."

Hell, yeah he had to hurry. He wouldn't lose his mate to the wolf without him taking his last breath.

Tristan called the shift to his body "Get the Aunts. Have them on alert for when I get back with her."

He completed his shift, as easy for him to do as breathing, his bones cracked, reshaped, and eventually realigned until he was wolf. After so many years of doing it, and six months when he'd been unable to shift back, his canine body was an easy fit for him. He leapt out the broken window after Ashlee. He would find her and bring her home. And then he was never letting her go.

He sniffed the ground. Ashlee had come in this direction and she had bled when she'd passed here. Injured?

No, not acceptable.

He raced forward as he followed her scent, each step he took her smell grew stronger. He sniffed the air. Damp earth, moldy leaves, wet vegetation and something else, Ashlee. As a human, Ashlee had smelled like vanilla beans and cinnamon. She still smelled of those things now but her wolf added to her the smell of pine leaves and fur. Yes, he was close.

He heard a whimper nearby and he whirled around. *Ashlee?*

Small vibrations on the ground behind him alerted him as she stepped out of the thick bushes. If he could have gasped, he would have at Ashlee's red and white coat. Very unusual. He'd never seen the like before. Her eyes bore into his before she dropped her gaze in submission and whimpered again. His wolf howled at its mate's distress. Tristan forced himself to focus. *Little Ashlee? You are a beautiful wolf. Can you hear me?*

Ashlee moaned.

You're hurt. Come to me. We'll shift back together and

get you healed.

Ashlee's wolf raised her eyes to him for a moment. *Alone.* Her voice was so soft in his head he barely heard it.

You're right, I left you alone. I'm sorry. I didn't know this would happen.

Her wolf blinked twice rapidly. Good, that meant she understood at least some of what he said.

Tristan?

That's right Ashlee. It's me. I've come for you.

You're still a wolf. The magic didn't work?

He shook his head. *It worked. I shifted back to find you. Come with me.*

She closed her eyes. *I hurt, Tristan.*

I know. We need to get you home and back to your other form.

How do we do that? I don't know how I became a wolf.

Come here.

Ashlee finally relented and stepped forward to him. She buried her nose in his fur and he shuddered. His wolf wanted free reign, but he couldn't allow it.

Mate? Her voice sounded strained.

I am your mate. You understand now.

I do. She closed her eyes.

No, no, no Ashlee. I am going to shift back and hold onto you. My magic should make you shift to a human as you are in my arms. Do you understand?

Tired.

I know you're tired. Please don't go to sleep. Internally

his wolf howled at him to not let her sleep. She'd lost so much blood. He bit down gently on her shoulder and she cried out in protest. He called his magic and felt it surround both of them. He took a deep breath. It would work, it had to. He felt his bones start to shift and Ashlee screamed. At first it was a harrowing howl of an animal in pain but quickly it was her own human voice. When he could, he wrapped his arms around her naked body. She trembled in his arms.

He held her tighter. "I've got you, I won't let you go. We'll get you fixed now."

She pulled back her head to look at him, dazed and slightly out of focus. He wiped the sweat off her brow and kissed her forehead. She was his to treasure and protect, given to him by fate as a gift, and he'd already let her get injured. Fury with himself welled up inside of him. She smiled weakly at him.

Her voice sounded hoarse. "I dreamed of you."

"You saw me as a man in your dream, not a wolf?" She nodded and closed her eyes. He looked down at her naked form and tried to force himself to catalog her injuries and not be distracted by her loveliness. Despite his best intentions, he did feel a pull in his groin. Ashlee's breasts were small and pert, perfect for her frame. He wanted to reach out and cup them, then lick the sweat from her body. His wolf howled at the thought. Yes he would stroke her with his tongue all the way from the bottom of her neck to the beautiful blonde hair that formed a V between her legs. He craved the taste of her, both on her skin and inside her beautiful folds where he knew heaven waited for him.

But he wasn't an animal, not entirely, and even his wolf knew it wasn't the time for that. He forced himself to focus on her wounds. Her hands were torn to shreds. Her sides looked raw and blood seeped out of a particularly bad wound.

She opened her eyes to stare at him. "I don't want to ever do that again." Her head fell backwards and her eyes rolled to the back under her eyelids.

"No, no, no." He picked her up in his arms and ran in the direction of the house. His brother should have found his Aunts by now. They would know how to fix this.

Ashlee first became aware of the sensation of drifting. She felt like she was on a slow moving raft that gently moved in the ocean. She was warm and cozy and didn't appreciate the voices that spoke to her. They tried to rip her from her quiet, peaceful raft.

"Why can't you just let her sleep?" Ah, Tristan, yes he understood. He would make them leave her alone.

"She needs fluids so we can bring down the fever. Wake her up, boy."

The woman's voice was unfamiliar to Ashlee. She was going to open her eyes up in a moment and kick her behind for talking so harshly to Tristan. Ashlee attempted to do just that but her eyes felt so heavy. Her eyelids fluttered but didn't open.

"Ashlee, can you hear me?" Tristan wanted her

attention but she just couldn't give it to him. The waiting warmth of her raft called to her and she went gladly.

The next time Ashlee awoke, it was to darkness. She forced her eyes open only to find that the room she slept in was nearly as dark as the inside of her eyelids had been. Her head pounded but she'd had worse headaches, her body felt achy and she couldn't really move.

The source of the last problem proved to be Tristan. He was asleep, his head pressed up against the back of hers, his arms wrapped around her body. She closed her eyes and forced her brain not to start coming up with reasons to be upset that he held her. It didn't work. They didn't really know each other. She'd only ever seen him as a human once. He'd told her she belonged to him, and that wherever she went, he would go, but he'd left her alone to face her first change by herself. None of that was enough for her to force him to move his arms so she decided to listen to him breathe for a while.

He didn't snore, that was a relief. If there was even a chance this was going to work, and it was a small chance at best, they'd need to be compatible in most ways. She'd never been able to tolerate a loud snorer. Contentment flowed through her as she tentatively stroked his arm. What she could remember from when she'd seen him as a human had confirmed her mother's earlier assertion that he was good looking. Attraction wasn't going to be a problem, at least on her end.

Tristan took a deep breath and pulled her closer

against him. Okay, now it was too tight. He was going to bruise one of her ribs. She took his large hands in hers and gently tried to loosen his grip on her side. He murmured something but didn't let go. Damn it, she was going to have to wake him.

"Tristan." Silence answered her. He'd been a lighter sleeper when he'd been a wolf. She tried again, this time louder. "Tristan."

"What?" He pulled her fully up against his body as he came awake, which hurt even more. She grunted and he let go and she pulled away from him just enough to get a little breathing room.

"Sorry, was I squishing you? I meant to stay awake, guess I fell asleep."

Ashlee took a good look at Tristan, and was surprised by how clearly in the darkness she could make him out. There he was--the man from her dream, the one who'd rescued her in the woods. His features were regal, his body hard and pressed up against hers. She shivered against him. He looked rumpled, sleepy, and sexy as hell. His hair was cut close to his head, its color a golden brown shade with red highlights like his wolf's fur. He had stubble strewn across his face and a dimple in his left cheek. In her dream, his brown eyes had been sad but now as she stared at him they were tired but happy. Specks of grey, the same she'd noticed when he'd been a wolf, dotted his irises.

In some ways it had been easier when he was a canine, she could just reach out and touch him whenever she wanted, in the same way you might pet a dog. Now he was all man, and she couldn't just stroke his face. Could she?

"I'm a little unsure of myself." She wasn't usually so bold. She swallowed and felt her cheeks grow red with embarrassed heat.

He nodded. "Me too."

"Really? You're a hundred years old, haven't you encountered just about every situation at this point?"

"I feel like I really am thirty again, it's a little bit like I've rewound the last seventy years." Ashlee watched him scrunch up his forehead. "I shouldn't have said that. You're very new to this. I need to treat you like a human girl, and I have next to no experience with that, but I gather it's important for you to have choices, that you not feel rushed or forced into something."

"It's true. I need to be my own person but I understand a little better now what's happening. When I was in the woods, I felt alone in the world and I knew I shouldn't feel that way. I should have a pack. Then you came and I could smell you. I knew you were mine just by the way you smelled. It called to me, fed my soul in a way I didn't understand when I hadn't ever been a wolf." She paused to consider her next words and was grateful he gave her the time to do so. "I still feel her with me, the wolf. I'm changed because of her, even now as a human."

Tristan nodded. "She'll always be with you now, she's been sleeping your whole life, now that she's awake you're going to have to fight her for dominance for a while, and then eventually you meld into one being where you are both always. Although sometimes I still let myself disappear into the wolf when I'm on all fours because I like the sensation. But he never disappears into me. He's way too dominant for that."

"I'm feeling bold and frank, I'm not usually either of those things."

"That's her then. I'm not surprised, she, or rather you, is an exquisite wolf. I've never seen one like you before. "

Ashlee put her hands in her lap and sat up straight. "So, since I'm in a truthful mood, I will tell you that while I'm not sure I want to be owned," Tristan opened his mouth but she kept speaking and didn't give him a chance to answer. "I don't know if I can go without smelling, touching, or having you around, so I think we're going to have to work something out."

"Your eyes just went wolf, little one."

Ashlee reached up to touch her eyes, they felt dry. She blinked twice and tried to clear them but it didn't help.

"Take a deep breath. She's just trying to protect you because she doesn't know how I took that speech. Reassure her I am not upset, and even if I were, I would never harm you."

Ashlee took a deep breath and closed her eyes. How was she supposed to reassure her wolf of anything? With her eyes closed, Ashlee could actually feel the wolf within her. A presence in her mind. Had it always been there?

All is well?

Her Wolf

Her wolf spoke soothingly in her mind. She opened herself up to its thoughts and feelings. The canine was relieved to be with her now, sorry that her change had come so violently, and glad that they were no longer alone. Also, she adored Tristan who she thought of as one entity and not man or wolf. Ashlee's wolf had already made her choice; she was with Tristan for the long run. She just wanted Ashlee to catch up.

Ashlee decided to answer her. *All is well.*

I gave you dreams. It was the only way to speak to you. We can see things others don't see yet.

Ashlee nodded. *I know.* Should she thank her? *Thank you for saving Tristan.*

He belongs to me too.

You thought you were crazy. You betrayed yourself when you let those people tell you that you were.

I know. She had denied her own truth, she'd let others define her. *It won't happen again. I feel like I know myself now.*

This was the declaration the wolf had been waiting for and she settled back down before she added one last thought. *If you forget, I will remind you.*

Ashlee opened her eyes. Tristan smiled at her.

"You did that fast."

"I actually kind of like her. She's very simple to understand, she craves loyalty and love. It's very easy to love a creature like that."

"She's not trying to dominate you?"

Ashlee shook her head. "At least not right now."

"Then yours is nicer than mine." He laughed aloud

and grimaced. "My wolf didn't think that was very funny and actually now that I've found you he is rather content and unobtrusive"

Ashlee dove forward and captured Tristan's mouth with hers. He froze and Ashlee wondered if he was stunned for a second but then he pulled her head closer to his so their lips pressed together more firmly. Maybe her wolf was more in control than she realized, because Ashlee had no idea what had come over her. She wasn't complaining--Tristan tasted fantastic. His lips moved over her own with a firmness that she loved. Then, he snaked his tongue past them and his taste burst in her mouth--mint and sex.

One of his hands held her securely against him, the other roamed her back to trace patterns with his fingertips under her shirt, against her skin. She trembled and her nipples hardened. The sensations made her breathless. She wanted him, inside of her now. She pulled her lips from his and pushed him down on the bed so she could climb on top of him. It seemed desperately important she have him right that second.

His body showed her he agreed. The bulge in his corduroy pants told her he was hard and ready, beckoned her to reach inside and see for herself. Desperate to touch him, Ashlee stroked his large shaft through the velvety fabric of his corduroys. He groaned and closed his eyes.

"Ashlee, if we do this," he spoke through gritted teeth. "It will complete the mating ritual. We'll be bound together. I don't want you to do this and not know the full implications." An ill-timed knock on the door stopped whatever response she would have made.

"Plenty of time to mate later, children. I need to check on the patient."

"Damn it." Tristan uttered a low curse and shoved his shirt into his pants. He stood up and Ashlee watched him try to adjust himself. It must have pained him because with a grimace on his face he turned to face the wall.

Ashlee looked down at herself. She was a disheveled mess but whoever was out there, and Ashlee actually had to suppress the urge to sniff to see if she recognized the scent, knew what they were doing in here. Feeling comfortable in her state of rumpled clothing, she sat on the bed.

"Ready to meet some more family?"

Ashlee cocked her head to the side. "They're related to me?"

"Everyone is pack, little Ashlee, we're all family here."

The knock pounded on the door again. "Stop fussing with yourself, boy, and open this darn door."

"She's charming, I assure you." Tristan gave her a crooked smile and walked to the door. "Please, won't you come in Auntie?"

He opened the door and a tall, striking woman walked into the room. She was at least six feet tall with long grey hair that stretched all the way down to her feet. An elastic rubber band secured it behind her head.

She wore huge glasses that covered most of her face, a calf-length purple skirt and a green tee-shirt that read "Rhode Island Rocks" across the front.

Ashlee had never seen anyone who looked like Tristan's aunt.

Tristan's Auntie put her hands on her hips. "So, you gave us quite a fright last night. The injury wouldn't have been so bad if your body wasn't already under a tremendous amount of strain from lack of nourishment."

"I know, I haven't been eating. But, I will from now on." Ashlee had been listening to the same speech from her mother for months but it seemed more important to listen to Auntie. With all of her bright colored clothes and her long crazy hair, she still came across as incredibly intimidating.

"Right. So let's have a look at you, Ashlee. And by the way, I have a name, despite this one's preference to call me Auntie. It's Clarinda and after I tend to you, I'm going to teach you to do what I can do so that my sister and I can finally kill ourselves."

Chapter Five

Tristan stood in the council chambers and listened to Michael's plans to capture and ultimately eliminate their father. It was good to be back with his twenty-eight pack mates. He would always be closest with his brothers but he'd known the others his whole life and cared about each of them. He knew he should care about the decisions they made but he couldn't focus on anything other than Ashlee's gorgeous body. More than anyone else in the room he had reason to want his father destroyed. But he couldn't help but think that, in a truly perverse way, he owed his patriarch a great debt.

If he hadn't been trapped in his wolf form and placed in the zoo, he would never have found his mate.

Not that he intended to stay out of the mission to eliminate his father—he just wasn't all that interested in planning and plotting at the moment. He sighed and looked at his watch again for the fifth time in five minutes. Ashlee was with the Aunts, who were trying to teach her how to harness her inner energy, something Tristan couldn't help her with. The pack might be male-dominated in its hierarchy but the females could do amazing things their Y-chromosome counterparts couldn't even imagine.

"I don't think I want a mate if she'll make me stare off into space, heartsick like a fifteen-year-old kid." Theo's remark snapped Tristan back into the present. Twenty-eight pairs of annoyed eyes bored into him.

Tristan hoped his voice sounded apologetic but he doubted it. "I'm sorry, did I miss something?"

Michael snorted. "You mean other than the last six months?'

Tristan rolled his eyes. "Other than that, yes."

"I asked you what you thought about the assault plan."

"I think whatever plan my Alpha comes up with is the right one for our pack."

"That's just the thing, Trip. As the only member of this pack with a mate, we feel that perhaps it is a sign from the fates that you should take over as Alpha. I've never officially been made our leader and maybe that's because it's always supposed to have belonged to you."

Tristan gawked at Michael. "You'll do anything to deny you're our Alpha, won't you?"

Michael opened his mouth and Tristan knew he was about to argue his point. Internally, Tristan braced for the encounter, expecting the argument to affect him badly. It had always made him a little ill to argue with his father. Their wolf sides hated any confrontation with the Alpha. But when Michael spoke, the sick feeling Tristan had anticipated never arose.

"I'm your big brother Tristan. I'll always be that. But let's face it, I got this job by default because I was born first. I don't have the skills to lead. I didn't even have a clue how to find you when you went missing. It took Rex to track you down."

Next to Michael Azriel laughed. "Wanna be Alpha, Rex?"

"Nope. *I'm* not the Alpha" Rex crossed his arms over his chest and stared at Tristan. In fact all of the eyes in the room were on him. Why the hell was everyone staring at him?

He cleared his throat. "Michael, when Dad did what he did, the job fell to you, You are the oldest. Our natural born leader."

Michael shook his head. "Dad wasn't the first born, Tristan." Michael's eyes bore in Tristan's. He'd never seen his brother struggle for words like this before. "He was the third son."

"And look how fabulous that turned out. Maybe it should have been the first born instead of our clinically insane father."

Tristan heard grumbles behind him but he didn't turn around to see what they muttered about.

"You're not Dad and when you were gone…we were lost."

"What the hell does that mean?" Now they were just starting to piss him off. If Michael had a point he needed to get to it.

"I'm not the Alpha. I know it. My wolf knows it. Everyone here knows it."

"You're just nervous because you don't want to be like Dad. You were born to do it."

Gabriel laughed, a cold hard sound, and stepped next to Michael. "What other reason should Michael be Alpha, Tristan, other than his birth order? Do you really think he's Alpha? Look inside of you, what do you see?" Gabriel dropped his eyes after he made that speech in a gesture of submission. Tristan whirled around and stared at his fellow pack-mates. Not one of them would meet his eyes. He had no idea what was going on but he was going to put an end to it now.

He opened his mouth to speak, to tell them they were all nuts and that anyone who didn't support Michael was as good as treasonous but any attempt to argue was forgotten as a grey and black wolf plowed into the group. Although no one would dare to complain, Cullen's arrival made the already tense situation worse. The white light that always accompanied the shift surrounded Cullen for a moment before his body stretched into his formidable human form. Tristan watched as Cullen strode to the back of the room and put on a pair of sweat pants and a tee-shirt that was always stored there.

Cullen Murphy, the oldest living wolf-shifter in their pack, stood just under six-feet tall, smaller than the Royals but what he lacked in height he made up for in strength and power. Tristan always thought Cullen resembled a bulldozer. He could knock into any potential enemy, hard, and in one swift movement, be done with them.

When Tristan had been a child, Cullen had been so terrifying Tristan had behaved at every pack meeting just so Cullen wouldn't turn his haunted gaze on him. Cullen had been his father's closest advisor. There were many in the pack that mistrusted him, and felt he still worked for their former Alpha. But Tristan didn't share that view. Although Cullen looked thirty years old like the rest of the unmated pack, his eyes were ancient. He'd been as betrayed as the rest of them.

"Much as I love these little discussions where the Royal Six argue like small children over the Alpha position, we have bigger problems." Cullen's gravel-filled voice was a trigger for Tristan. Just one second of listening to it and Tristan wasn't a man with nearly a century under his belt, but a terrified kid of five who had snuck out to watch the pack perform death rites on a member whose wife had passed on. Tristan closed his eyes for a moment in respect to the memory.

Michael stood silently for a moment in front of Cullen. "And what would the more important matters be? Perhaps you'd like to be Alpha? Too bad your blood doesn't hold the requisite magic to live endlessly after finding your mate, or we'd all be thrilled to pass the job on to you."

Cullen raised one eyebrow which, Tristan realized, was akin to other people rolling their eyes. "Please don't mistake my interest in this pack's survival with a desire to take over your position, my interim-Alpha." Tristan tried not to smile. It was hard to dress down Michael but Cullen did it every time he showed up.

Tristan watched Michael storm to the window and look outside. He spoke without turning around. "Get on with it, Cullen. Your arrival back from Mexico can only mean you bring news of our father." Tristan took a deep breath. If Cullen did bring news of their father, it would mean the time had come to go and destroy Kendrick, the royal six's sire. As their father's former second-in-command, Cullen had taken on the quest to find and destroy him as a personal vendetta. The job was what kept Cullen alive. It was rumored he had lived four hundred years now without a mate. Most shifters chose to perform the ritual suicide after less time, feeling hopeless without a mate.

But not Cullen. He'd lived as their Alpha's second, a bogeyman for the pack's children, and now as a potential assassin, for longer than Tristan could imagine. If Cullen was at all interested in telling stories, Tristan was sure they could learn a great deal from him, but Cullen was never willing to share or instruct. He was more likely to terrorize and destroy.

"There's movement inside the facility. He seems to

be bringing people in. Several of his flunkies left about a month ago and haven't returned. I think it would behoove us to find out what they want." Cullen crossed his hands over his chest while he stared at Michael's back.

"Was it three men? The blond man with the snake tattoo and two others?" Tristan asked to break up the silence that had taken over the room.

Cullen nodded. "Yes. How did you know that, Prince Tristan?" Inwardly, Tristan flinched at the title. His father had insisted on nonsense like rank and order but he and his brothers had never held to it.

"They attacked me and my mate two days ago after she rescued me from the zoo I was being held in."

Cullen stared at him. "I think I've missed quite a bit."

Tristan thought it was perhaps the first time he'd ever seen Cullen befuddled before. He tried not to laugh.

Michael turned from the window. "We've been trying to contact you for some time. You need to start carrying a cell phone."

"As I am watching the facility as a wolf, there isn't really a place to carry a cell phone."

Michael made a noise that was something between a growl and a laugh. "Surely you must go somewhere to sleep for the night, some place where you shower. You can leave the cell phone there and check your messages so at least I can tell you when my brother has been kidnapped and we fear him dead, or when he's returned with his mate in tow. Surely Tristan is important enough to warrant that much respect from you."

Cullen nodded and Tristan snorted which earned him a glare from Michael. Tristan had never seen Cullen acquiesce to anything before.

"How did you get away from the three attackers, Prince Tristan?"

Tristan itched to correct him about the prince title but he'd long ago ceased trying.

"Rex, Victoria, and I killed them outside the zoo where I'd been held."

"Victoria is your mate?" Cullen shouted and Tristan blinked in surprise.

"Ah…no, although I don't know why that would surprise you so greatly. Her eldest daughter Ashlee is my mate."

"Victoria has a daughter? The young woman who drove me to distraction with her hysterical actions, is mated and mother of your mate?"

It had never occurred to Tristan that any of the antics he and the others had pulled as young pack members had affected Cullen at all. They'd seemed below his notice.

"Victoria has two daughters and she is mated to a plastic surgeon in New Jersey who knows all about us. However, until two days ago his eldest daughter did not know anything about her heritage and her younger one still does not."

Cullen looked around the room. "Do you think

you found your mate because the danger has finally passed, so Mary Jo's spell is finally voided?"

"Either that or I really was just in the right place at the right moment." Tristan didn't know. Metaphysical questions had never been his area of interest. When it came to pack dynamics, he preferred to be his brother's advisor, a dominant warrior, and now Ashlee's mate. Although right now, he could kill his brothers for their indecision. The pack needed strength and security. He would never be able to fulfill his role as advisor if Michael never fully took on his Alpha position. Hell, if he wasn't so completely unfit for the position—hadn't his father told him so a million times?—he'd take it on himself. Outside of the pack, he painted and sold his artwork. As far as Tristan was concerned, the mystics could take care of the pack's magical needs without his involvement.

Something about his last thoughts bothered Tristan. His father had told him more than he could count that he would make a lousy Alpha. Why had he done that? Tristan's skin started to crawl.

"Where is your mate now?"

"What?" Tristan's attention was thrown back to the present. Figuring out why his father had been so adamant he'd never be Alpha would have to wait until later.

Cullen lowered his eyes. Why was everyone doing that? "Where is your mate now, Prince Tristan?"

"Last time I saw her, the Aunts were driving her crazy. I think she's trying to digest a lifetime of study and knowledge before lunch."

Theo cut into their discussion reminding Tristan he was in a room with twenty-eight other people besides Cullen and himself. "You never mentioned a sister."

"Victoria isn't going to give her to us until she is at least Ashlee's age and not until she's had the chance to finish school. The girls were both raised as humans. Ashlee is taking this all pretty well, but Victoria isn't ready to limit the sister's options just for our convenience."

Theo laughed, hard and loud. "Does she understand we have been living here in agony for thirty years with no women? Not any?"

Across the room, Michael grimaced. "We did have the Aunts."

As if on cue, the chamber door burst open and Tristan's two aunts entered, followed by Ashlee. The very sight of her took his breath away. All other spectacles and sounds in the room faded and he realized how Ashlee's mother could have lived off-island for as long as she did. Tristan could live anywhere, do anything, and be anyone that Ashlee needed. She smiled at him and he grinned back.

She was a precious gift he didn't deserve but one he was going to keep anyway. Others had suffered much more than he; the bloodshed that had followed the spell the witch placed on the island had been devastating for Tristan. He'd lost his mother to a violent death perpetrated by his father. Even though he'd been seventy years old and well past the point of childhood, he'd lost his innocence.

Now he really understood the full magnitude of what had happened that day. Members of his pack had awoken from what felt like a drunken sleep to find they had murdered their mates. Tristan could actually feel the anguish they had felt that day because he knew beyond a shadow of a doubt that if he ever harmed even a hair on Ashlee's head, the pain he would suffer would go beyond all physical agony he had ever endured.

Something on his face must have given away his thoughts because Ashlee's eyes narrowed and she looked at him with concern. She thought something was wrong with him. He blinked and tried to cheer up. He was lucky. He could look forward to being with Ashlee for the rest of his life, an existence that finally had a determinable end-date.

Relief surged through Ashlee's body when she saw Tristan's mood brighten. If her presence brought on that amount of darkness to his features, she would stay away from him. Except she found that ever since she'd jumped his bones in his bedroom earlier, she couldn't seem to stop craving him. If he was a drug, she was addicted.

Tristan's aunts, Clarinda and Adeline, had spent the entire morning teaching her about pack dynamics and trying to get her to 'feel the mystic within.' Ashlee learned the pack rules rather easily, some of it felt intuitive, as if she already knew it and the rest she absorbed without any problems. But awakening her magic was another matter. If Ashlee was any judge, she didn't have any magic to awaken. But the aunts were persistent. They told her a young woman who could become a wolf all on her own by just stepping foot onto Westervelt must be filled to the brink with untapped abilities. They had been very patient with her, which Ashlee appreciated.

If Clarinda's style of dress was eccentric and eclectic at best, Adeline looked like she'd walked out of a New York City fashion show. Her hair, dyed black—Ashlee could see her grey roots—was slicked back with mousse and cut close to her head. The sleeveless, mustard yellow shift dress she wore showed off her shapely arms that had to take a tremendous amount of work to maintain. Red pumps and black silk stockings finished off the outfit; not colors Ashlee would have put with mustard yellow but it worked for the older woman.

When they decided it was time for Ashlee to meet the rest of the pack, they'd dragged her across the Institute to the meeting chambers where she now stood feeling like the new kid in school who the teacher made stand up and speak to the class. Tristan walked over to her and put his arm around her waist. She knew she should want to be more independent and not labeled as 'his woman' but she liked it. Her wolf, who had gotten more and more vocal as the day went on, liked it too. Tristan had said eventually she and the wolf would become one unit, and Ashlee could see how that would work better than this constant discussion between the two of them about the proper ways to behave.

Tristan smiled at the group. "This is Ashlee. She rescued me from the zoo in New Jersey. She is my mate, and as most of you know, she changed into a wolf by herself without any outside help."

Ashlee felt her cheeks heat. "The last bit was entirely not my own doing. Believe me, I would rather have not gone through that alone." Laughs met her remark and she was relieved to see almost everyone in the room looked at her with a friendly demeanor. Theo still appeared somewhat hostile, but maybe that was just the way he looked most of the time. A man she didn't know stood in the circle next to Michael, look at her with a demeanor of distance the others didn't share.

"We were just discussing the plans to go after my father. Cullen," Michael indicated the man next to him who'd given her the distant appraisal, "was just telling us our father's headquarters has been active and on the move."

"He has a headquarters?" Ashlee was confused. Why hadn't they eliminated him by now if they knew where he was?

Michael nodded. "He and some of his less-than-reputable medical partners run a mental health facility in Mexico where they perform unnecessary medical procedures on the criminally insane. Tristan just told us you met three of his former patients outside of the zoo before you came here."

A vision of Snake-man plunged into her mind. His sick smile, the half of his face designed to look like a serpent. Ashlee hadn't thought of him since they'd left him dead in the parking lot. Just the thought of his face chilled her to the bone. Tristan's father had experimented on him, had made him that way, and now they wanted Tristan.

No one was safe on this island, not by a long shot.

Suddenly, Ashlee needed to know all the details of Tristan's imprisonment. "Tristan, how did you get caught in the first place?"

"Rex and I drove into Portland to get some supplies that we needed."

"Tristan wanted watercolors and I ran out of Yuengling Lager." Rex cut off Tristan's story.

"Don't lie," Tristan spat. "You wanted more than beer, Rex. He loves music and can spend endless hours in that used CD store on Fore Street. After waiting an hour and a half, I finally had enough of his musings about Nirvana and Garbage so I told him I would go to the art supply store myself and meet in front of Gritty McDuff's pub down the block. I waited outside the pub for twenty minutes before I was jumped. I assumed they had Rex so I fought back, instead of losing them which is the protocol in cities or around large crowds of people. I thought I could rescue him. But they struck me with this spell. It felt like worms crawled all over my body, and I shifted against my will. We must have made a commotion, because people came pouring out of the pub. Dad's men ran off. Then I ran because I wasn't going to be any good for Rex stuck as a wolf. I don't know where I actually went but when I woke up

Her Wolf

I was in the back of an animal control car on my way to New Jersey."

Ashlee blanched at the way Tristan told the story, his voice devoid of any emotion. She realized that at some point during that drive, Tristan must have become convinced Rex betrayed him to his father. It wasn't polite but she was going to ask him about it.

"After the fight in the parking lot, you acted like Rex had betrayed you. Why?"

"The longer I stayed in that cage, the more I became convinced he must have told them where I was because he was the only one who knew I was in Portland that day and where I would be."

Rex shook his head. "It wasn't me. I was late, I'm always late. I missed you by fifteen minutes. I caught your scent, I knew you had shifted, I could smell it. I knew you would never have done that in the middle of Portland if you'd had a choice. I followed your scent for miles before I lost you. So I called Michael and we decided I would go hide out at Dad's facility and see if you showed up there. When those three goons left last week, I followed them and ended up in New Jersey." Rex was silent for a second but the look on his face, the way his eyebrows slanted down led Ashlee to believe he wasn't done talking, "I knew you would think I betrayed you, but I hoped you knew better."

Cullen, the distant one, stared at Rex. "I never smelled you at the facility."

"I smelled you and if I could, I knew Dad could too. I stayed the hell away, I didn't want him recognizing me."

"But why couldn't I pick up your scent?"

"You're not the only one with tricks, old man." Rex's tone was jovial but his eyes had gone wolf. Ashlee swallowed remembering how he'd done that on the boat too. Rex must let his wolf loose more often than the others. Cullen made a growling noise in his throat.

"Alright." Michael interrupted their display. "You're both big men. For the moment, I'm in charge here and I say enough. Ashlee's going to take Trip and run out of here faster than any of us can imagine if we don't all start to behave like civilized people."

Ashlee opened her mouth to object but then closed it as her wolf growled at her.

Alpha.

Ashlee wasn't sure what that meant, but she had a feeling it was her wolf's way of telling her not to argue with the boss.

"Trip, you're no good to me like this, all gooey and doe-eyed. I want my warrior back. So take your mate and get the ritual done so we can have you back. Tonight we run as a pack. I want Ashlee integrated now. Then tomorrow we meet and figure out a game plan for dealing with Dad and the witch. Cullen I expect you to stay and run with the pack. No disappearing right now." Michael nodded to everyone and left the room.

"Why doesn't he just become the full-fledged Alpha?" Ashlee whispered to Tristan.

Tristan looked at the floor. "Because he's afraid, as we all are, that we're too much like Dad. That the power of the Alpha, after the ceremony, is so intense he'll go mad with it like Dad did and betray everyone we love."

"Your father did that to you on purpose. He kept the six of you weak so you'd never be a real threat to him. I didn't realize that's what he was doing at the time, I didn't realize a lot of things about our former leader, but that's what he did. But your mother made you strong. Just look for her power." Cullen's voice from right behind her startled Ashlee so much she jumped. Tristan put his hand on her shoulder to steady her as Cullen tuned on his heel and left the room.

"He's a bit much, isn't he?" Ashlee watched Cullen stalk from their sight.

"He can be, yes. He's the bogeyman to the wolf children. Don't misbehave at pack meetings, listen to your Alpha, don't betray our secrets, or Cullen will come and get you. He actually came and got me once when I'd disobeyed. Needless to say I never disobeyed again."

"What did he do to you?" Ashlee asked as images of dark dungeons and beatings filled her head.

"He made me do manual labor for a month. This place shined like a new penny when I was done scrubbing it."

So Cullen was tough but not brutal. Ashlee could respect that.

"One more thing, Tristan, what is the mating ritual we need to get done so you can stop being doe-eyed?"

"Michael just ordered us to go have sex."

That's what she'd thought. If her cheeks were as red as she thought they were, she was the color of a tomato.

Chapter Six

"What about this one?"

Tristan smiled. The painting Ashlee pointed to was his favorite. She'd been walking around his room asking him about every one of his creations. He couldn't imagine being more happy than he was right at this moment.

"That was one of the first I did in watercolor. I wasn't even sure I could use a brush. All of my work before that had been in charcoal."

He'd sat outside for hours and watched the chickens in his mother's yard cluck and peck their way through their food supply for the day. He captured two of them from memory during their feeding. It was a very simple picture, just two chickens being chickens but it had proven to him that he could paint with a brush.

Ashlee turned from examining the painting to smile at him. He reached out and touched the side of her face. Tristan watched as she closed her eyes for a second and then opened them again. Yep, this was happiness.

"Why was all your previous work in charcoal?"

"I trained in architecture. The Institute was my design." She beamed at him and he felt like he grew taller by two inches. "So when I started trying to do art that wasn't building design, I immediately went to charcoal because I could hold the block of charcoal like I held a pencil. "

"Do you still do architectural design?"

Tristan shook his head. "No. The last time I designed something was eighty years ago. It's all very different now. I can use a computer as well as anyone, but I've never even tried the software." Tristan swallowed. "But, if you want to leave here, to go live somewhere else, I'll do that, go back to school. Learn the new stuff and start over with another architecture career."

She looked at him, her right eyebrow raised and Tristan wished he could read her mind. That might have been a useful trick to give mates, the power of mind reading.

"What makes you think I want to leave here?"

He didn't mind the question. At least she wasn't denying they'd be together.

"I'm just letting you know I'll go wherever you want." He gulped. He had meant that when he said it earlier but now something seemed to be changing inside of him. He would do whatever Ashlee wanted but he couldn't seem to shake the feeling that they needed him here. What had Michael meant when he'd said they'd been lost without him?

Do you really not know?

Was that annoyance he heard in his wolf's voice? *What do you mean?*

He thought he heard the creature sigh. *Never mind it now.*

"I wanted to go into interior design. I paint too." Ashlee grinned at him.

Tristan's heart jumped. "Wow. That's incredible." Inside, his wolf leapt with delight, their strange conversation from moments earlier forgotten instantly. He wanted to shift to four feet and leap in the air. He settled for just inhaling Ashlee's unique scent. Cinnamon and vanilla. He'd noticed it when he'd been stuck in the wolf enclosure and he drowned in the glory of it now.

"I don't know if I want to live in your bedroom for the rest of my days. There's no where to put my stuff."

Inside, his wolf dropped down on all fours in disgust. *Idiot.*

He'd had ample time to clear out some drawers for her, why didn't he? He didn't use the smallest bit of the manners his mother had taught him. His mate was currently living out of a suitcase.

She grabbed his hands and pulled them out of his hair. "I'm not saying I'm unhappy. I think we can make room for me in here. But… well, I thought that I saw some old, decrepit-looking cottages on the south side of the island when I walked with the Aunts today…" she trailed off, seeming unsure.

He knew the ones, they'd all gone to ruin thirty years ago when the insanity had descended on the island. The remaining unmated males had all moved into the Institute and let their childhood homes fall apart. It had seemed appropriate, as their lives before the spell had been destroyed too.

"I want you to build me a cottage. I don't want to live here, in your dorm-like bedroom, forever. I want a home. A real home."

Tristan wanted to leap again. "Yes, I can do that, little Ashlee. I'll build it myself, with my own two hands. Our home, yes."

"Sometimes, when you get really excited, the way you say things becomes old fashioned. It's adorable." Her eyes were playful, her grin a sexual taunt if he'd ever seen one. His groin grew hard.

"We can't have babies. But maybe we can bring this place back to life." The playfulness left her eyes as she spoke.

"I really don't care about that. I don't need children. I'm not even sure I like them. Besides, I'd rather not have to share your attention." He wasn't lying; he wouldn't have minded having kids someday but it wasn't a must-have. He felt so blessed with Ashlee in his life he wouldn't trade her for a million children.

Her eyes were so serious it almost stopped his heart. "I believe you, but you have to understand…when my fiancé found out I couldn't have babies, he got so upset he ran out and had sex with the counter chick from the local Dairy Queen. Ironically, that little indiscretion got her pregnant and I became so distraught over it I had a nervous breakdown, dropped out of college, and terrified my parents." Tristan watched as Ashlee suddenly became interested in her shoes. She had been worried about telling him of her past. "I can't help but have this belief that men want women who can have their offspring. You and I are part animal and animals want to procreate."

He walked the few steps to her and pressed his body up against hers. She moved backwards until she was halted by the wall behind her. "You and I are sentient beings, humans, who have this special gift inside of us, an ability most do not have. It makes us loyal, attentive, and family-oriented but we're still human beings. You are mine. Period. I wouldn't care if you were missing a limb, I'd still want you like I do now, and I'd like to think if there was an equivalent problem with me, you'd feel the same way." He leaned down until his mouth was just above hers. "Little Ashlee, you are my mate--after tonight you will always be with me. I've never been mated, obviously, but I'm told it's very intense."

He pressed his mouth to hers and lost all coherent thought.

Ashlee ran her hands up Tristan's sculpted arms as his tongue conquered her mouth. Their lips met again and again and their tongues invented games to play. She wanted to be closer to him so she didn't stop her hips when they ground hard into his. He pulled his mouth from hers and then crushed it down to hers with a passion that she loved.

Mine. Her wolf smiled, a big canine grin.

Ours. Ashlee corrected her.

But then, all of her focus was on Tristan. The feelings that just kissing Tristan aroused in her body were unlike anything she had ever felt before. Her nipples hardened under her shirt and she wanted the offensive material off, now. Tristan seemed to understand her desires. He picked her up and carried her to the bed. He kissed her one more time, hard, then pulled the shirt from her body. Buttons flew and fabric ripped as he threw the shirt into the corner. Tristan ran his hands up from her stomach to her breasts. She shuddered under his touch and he grinned at her. She was going to have a lifetime to see that smile but she knew she'd never forget how it looked right this moment. Tristan's appreciative grin was sincere, focused, and adoring.

She reached up to pull his shirt from his body, but ultimately he had to help her. Her hands shook and she couldn't make them work. Shirtless, he reached down and took one of her fingers in his mouth. He sucked, hard and she thought she might die from the pleasure.

HER WOLF

Her panties, that had already been wet, were suddenly soaked. He inhaled sharply and she blushed. He seemed to want to be even closer, he pressed his nose over the apex of her thighs and took a long deep breath before he brushed his nose over the top of her pants.

They were wolves, they could smell each other's arousal. The more turned on Tristan got, the more he smelled of musk and heat, the kind of hotness she'd only known from a sauna. It was a total turn-on.

She was embarrassed. She'd just drenched her underwear, and he knew it. From the grin on his face, he loved it so she decided not to worry about it and to lose herself in the moment. It wasn't a hard task as he pulled her bra off and took one of her nipples in his mouth. She made a sound that must have been a whimper, he grunted in response.

Why was she so fortunate? What had she ever done to deserve to be touched in such an intense manner by such an extraordinary man?

Still on top of her, he pulled her pants from her body, followed immediately by his own. Ashlee took a moment to admire Tristan's nearly naked physique. He could have been sculpted from stone, his muscles were chiseled and she could see his hard shaft pushing through his tight blue briefs. She reached out to grab the tip of it through the cotton and he hissed. Ashlee pulled his briefs off and he followed suit by removing hers. They were both in a complete state of undress and she was so hot she was afraid she might set off the smoke alarms if he didn't touch her immediately.

She pressed her mouth back to his. She missed his taste on her tongue. Tristan growled, a sound that was all wolf, and her animal responded. If she'd been part cat, she would have purred, but being a wolf, she started rubbing his body instead. Up and down around his neck, his stomach, his abdomen—anywhere she could reach she stroked him with her tongue. Tristan closed his eyes and threw his head backwards for a second before he growled again and pushed her down on the bed, his body pressed on top of hers.

Ashlee gripped Tristan's shoulders tight and squirmed with pleasure at the feel of his body heat melting over hers. Her body throbbed everywhere now. Tristan reached down and touched her wet core with his hand.

"Oh god, Ashlee, you are so wet, I love it."

He took his finger coated with her pleasure and sucked it in his mouth.

"Hmm." He closed his eyes.

"Tristan?" Ashlee wasn't sure what she asked for, she'd never been this turned on before, she'd thought she'd had orgasms, felt real pleasure. She'd been wrong. Inside of Ashlee, her wolf squirmed and begged for more—more scents, more tastes, more... Tristan—and he obliged, leaning back down and stroking her hard, throbbing clit with his hands. Her hips rose off of the bed in answer. His fingers slid inside her, and their sexual play drove her crazy. A pressure built inside of her. Never, never had she felt anything so intense. She thought she might explode from it.

Ashlee's head thrashed back and forth on the bed. She sucked in her breath. "Tristan, please, I can't."

"You can." His intense voice, had lowered an octave and it sent shivers throughout her body. Fingers slid in and out, over and over. She exploded. Ashlee saw stars before her eyes. Inside and out, Ashlee came around his fingers.

Tristan moaned while on top of her. His kiss swallowed every cry that fell from her lips. While she still shivered, he entered her, one fluid, strong movement and he filled her. Ashlee's sheath had to stretch to accommodate the size of him. It was a glorious pull, her body soon made space for him and every inch of Tristan brought tingles of pleasure throughout her body.

"Tristan…you're so huge." Ashlee couldn't believe the sexy purr that was her own voice.

"You were made for me. As you can see we were made for each other." Tristan's long stroke inside of her brought on a groan. "Oh god, Ash, I can hardly breathe for wanting you so badly."

Tristan picked up the pace of his thrusts and Ashlee moaned with excitement. Feeling wanton, she slid her hands down his back to grasp his hard, toned ass.

"You're bad, Ashlee. I'm going to love doing this with you forever."

Forever. Just yesterday that would have terrified her. But since she'd woken up this morning and met her wolf, Tristan's promise of forever felt exactly right. He would never leave her. Tristan kissed her cheeks and she realized tears rolled down them.

She started to come again and right at that moment they were both bathed in a warm, white light. She felt her body's release and Tristan's followed moments after. She felt like she was floating in pure light, she and Tristan together. A soothing calmness overcame her. Her thoughts seemed to flow out of her and into Tristan's mind even as his entered hers. Is this what they meant by mating ritual, why it was more than just lovemaking?

She could hear Tristan in her mind. Pieces of his soul entered her body and took root there. For the first time in her life she felt complete. There was no gaping wound of insecurity, no feelings of being less than what she should be. Tristan filled her. At the same time she could tell the same thing happened to Tristan. He closed his eyes, his mouth forming a smile. Whatever pieces of her he had received, he liked them. She closed her eyes and tried to determine what parts of Tristan's soul would now reside with her.

Deep within her she could feel Tristan's soul show itself. Loyalty it was coded in her psyche now, a deep blue line she could find if she searched for it. His intensity—no surprise, it was a cardinal red, his belief system, his unerring optimism. His love of her—this last one was the thickest cord, it was black and if the others resembled silk, this one was steel rope. They attached her to Tristan and they flowed from his soul into hers.

"You didn't tell me this was going to happen." She

teased him because she knew she could. She knew beyond a shadow of a doubt now Tristan would always love her, never leave, and be forever loyal to her.

"I didn't know. No one ever talks about the mating ritual. It's considered to be very private, I can see why. My Ashlee, you have the most beautiful soul."

She closed her eyes, content to just float with him in the white light and the colored cords they'd made together until it passed, and if it never did, that was fine by her too.

Tristan's eyes flew open. When had they fallen asleep? It didn't matter, the white light was gone and in its place was pain. Unbelievable, unbearable pain. It filled his very pore, dripped from his eyelids, made his belly turn.

Something needed to relieve this pain. Something, anything, someone tell him how he could make it stop.

Kill her.

Who had said that? Not his wolf. No his wolf howled inside of him, it needed relief too.

Very simple. The pain will stop, when you kill her. Kill her, Tristan.

He knew that voice. It was his father, his Alpha. His father was still his Alpha right? Something was wrong but the pain, it stopped him from thinking clearly. He couldn't focus on any one thing, couldn't make sense out of senselessness.

But his Alpha spoke to him and told him what to

do, ordered him to take action.

Kill her, Tristan. Obey me.

Ashlee's eyes fluttered open to stare at him. Her beautiful green eyes smiled at him in his frenzy.

Do it. Do it. Do it. Do it. Do it.

He gripped his head and rolled onto the floor. He shut his eyes. No, he didn't want to. There had to be another way to stop the pain. He screamed, but he didn't know if it was just in his head. Ashlee's arms came around him.

"Tristan, what is it? What's going on?" Her voice sounded scared but he didn't dare open his eyes to look at her.

Kill her. Obey your Alpha.

"Ashlee," he barked. "I need you to run or I'm going to kill you." He pulled a deep breath into his lungs, trying to fight the sick, heavy fog that swamped his mind "I have to obey my Alpha. Run, baby, run now and hide from me. Don't let me find you."

Pain knifed through him and he felt like he was being gutted. Bright lights danced behind his closed eyelids. A fog formed over his mind and tried to put him into a deep sleep. He fought back but the command to obey was strong. He felt a tear escape his eye and his wolf howled inside of him not to give in, to fight the pain, not to kill her. He could barely hear his constant companion. Ashlee let go of Tristan's body, and he heard her run into the hall. Good, he had wanted that, hadn't he?

Ashlee needed to die and he would see to it. Then

he could rest, and then the pain would stop. If she wanted to run, he would chase her. He was a wolf after all. He called the shift to himself, and he followed his mate.

Kill her.
Yes, my Alpha, I will.

Chapter Seven

Ashlee tore into the hallway from their bedroom like the hounds of hell were after her. And the scariest part was that wouldn't be far from the truth. Her bare feet hit the ground hard as she forced her sleep-deprived, recently sated body to move faster. Something had happened to Tristan and Ashlee had no idea what it was. But he'd told her to run, told her he would kill her if he found her. Her wolf's ears pulled back and inside she whimpered. Tristan was in pursuit. Her wolf could sense him.

If he catches me, I'm dead. But even worse—he is too.

HER WOLF

She possessed part of Tristan's soul now. If he murdered her, he would then be compelled to take his own life as well, and he would never forgive himself for her pain. She could not let that happen.

She rounded the corner, her hands scraping at the walls. Every step, every ragged breath put more distance between her and Tristan. Or so she hoped.

She screamed as loudly as she could. She wasn't even sure what she said but the further she ran, the more she bellowed. He was getting closer, in a moment he would catch her. Her heart pounded and she gasped for breath. She could smell his approach. Just moments earlier Tristan's scent—the forest, the breeze, and the water—would have meant heaven to Ashlee. Now it terrified her.

Theo and Rex ran into the corridor. Ashlee had just seconds to take in their appearance. Theo was half-dressed, shirtless, and the expression on his face said he wasn't happy to have been disturbed. Rex looked exactly like he had earlier at their meeting but now he held a beer bottle in his left hand. She careened into Rex's arms.

Rex almost fell backwards as Theo questioned her. "What is it?"

"It's Tristan—he woke up and now he wants to kill me. He told me to run right before he lost control. Help him, you have to help him," Ashlee panted out each word, as she struggled to catch her breath. Her wolf howled for release, to be allowed to shift, she wanted her mate back, and she wanted Tristan. Ashlee's eyes filled with tears, she wanted the same thing.

Rex set her on the ground and shoved her next to him. "Did you perform the mating ritual?"

Ashlee nodded. It felt wrong to even voice that answer. The time between them had been so private. It dawned on her suddenly what Rex had just asked—he didn't want to know if they'd had sex. He thought the spell had come back, that Tristan had been afflicted with the endless desire to kill her, as his kin had been thirty years earlier. Was that it, was that what happened? Ashlee let out a half-sob and covered her mouth with her hands.

"Shit." Theo screamed. "He's right around the corner. We'll head him off. Ashlee, Trip is fierce, deadly. Our father trained him and Gabriel as assassins when he was Alpha. It's likely he will overpower Rex and me in a matter of moments. Get to Gabriel and Michael. They are two floors up. Take the stairs, run, now."

This was the second time today she'd been told to flee and once again she obeyed. Ashlee turned towards the stairs and sprinted. She heard growls behind her and even though she knew it was stupid, when she reached the stair landing she turned around to look at the scene as it unfolded. Her wolf didn't give her any other choice. She wanted to see her mate, and just as strongly, she didn't want any of the other pack members to get hurt on her behalf.

Stay.

Her wolf begged. Ashlee was surprised to see that she agreed. She wasn't going leave others to this. If this was to be her fate, she would face it with dignity. She sucked in her breath. That hadn't been her own thought, it was Tristan's. It was the part of his soul that she now shared speaking to her. Tristan would not run from danger and now neither would Ashlee.

Theo and Rex had shifted into their wolf forms. Theo was brown with stripes of silver fur intertwined, Rex all black as she'd seen him that night at the zoo. When Tristan appeared before them, the length of time it took him was a tribute to how long he'd held himself back from stalking her.

Theo and Rex growled in unison. In response, Tristan bared his teeth and snarled. Tristan raised his head to look past them at her where she stood in the landing. She could see the saliva drip from his mouth and hit the floor. His eyes spoke of menace and the hard set of his jaw made Ashlee gasp. She didn't need to be a mind reader to know what he'd come for. He wanted her dead. Ashlee swallowed and pushed herself to be brave.

She stepped forward. "Tristan, you don't want to hurt your brothers."

Tristan growled louder and lunged forward. Theo intercepted him, used his own body to block Tristan's way to Ashlee. They snarled and ripped at each other. Fleetingly, Ashlee realized she would have to rethink her opinion of Theo. He'd come off so cold, so brusque but whatever else he might be, he was the type of man to put his body, without thought, between a woman and the man who wanted to kill her. Even when the man was his own brother.

"Stop it, Tristan." Ashlee shouted, her voice sounded hysterical to her own ears. Her face felt tight. She clenched her fists at her side.

Tristan pulled off of Theo and the two backed up and circled each other in fight positions. Rex growled, the hair on his back stood up. He would attack Tristan next, Ashlee's wolf knew what would happen. If Tristan was attacked on both sides, he would kill his attackers. She was sure about it and even if they then found a way to stop this madness, Tristan would never be okay again.

At that moment, the stair door swung open behind her. Ashlee was suddenly aware of the amount of noise they made because Michael, Gabriel, and Azriel poured through the door one after another, each panting. They must have been drawn to the sounds of the fight. Ashlee watched as Gabriel assessed the scene and within seconds the wolf appeared in his eyes. According to Theo he might actually be able to take him down. Less than a minute later, the Aunts and the remote man they called Cullen followed through the door.

"Everyone is here, Tristan," Ashlee whispered, crouching down to the floor to act non-threatening.

"Oh god, not again." Adeline screamed. "Not like Chester." Adeline's husband had been Chester, Ashlee had learned that the day before. He had killed himself rather than kill her, although from her desperation to end her own life it seemed to Ashlee she might have preferred the other option.

"Quiet." Ashlee commanded everyone. "Tristan, you don't want to kill me. You told me to run, you're in there somewhere." Tears filled Ashlee's eyes but she didn't let them fall. It wasn't the time for hysterics but her eyes burned from the effort to hold them back. "Neither of us has to die. We can beat this. Do you hear me? What we just shared, it makes us stronger. The others, they didn't know what happened, they couldn't reason through it. But we know the past, we know the events of thirty years ago. We can beat this now. You told my mother you were your mother's son, not your father's. She foiled your Dad, her Alpha, thirty years ago. Let's destroy him now too."

A white light swept over Tristan and he changed back into his human form. He writhed on the ground, naked and Ashlee had to resist every primal instinct she possessed and stop herself from running over to him. She swallowed hard; her mouth was so dry, her throat hurt.

"Brother," Tristan called out to Theo. "Please, brother, I beg you. Kill me or give me something to get the job done myself. Please…it is too painful. I cannot take anymore. It is eating my brain, devouring me from the inside out. Please."

Theo turned around to them and Ashlee saw him blink away tears.

Michael stepped forward. "If you kill yourself, brother, you will doom Ashlee to follow or live a half-life like our Aunts have all these years. You do not want that. You and Ashlee are our salvation. If you die, all hope will be lost. I am your Alpha, I command you hold on."

"Ha! You are not my Alpha." Drool escaped Tristan's mouth as he rolled over on to his stomach. He tried to stand up and failed. "You have never been willing to be my Alpha, you cannot claim to be now. Do the ceremony if you want the respect."

Ashlee stepped towards Tristan and he jerked off the floor as if he was possessed. He rolled over and groaned. "Knock him out, Gabriel. Don't kill him, just render him unconscious and then we will lock him up where he cannot hurt himself while we figure out what to do to rid him of this."

Gabriel looked to Michael for confirmation, who nodded. As Gabriel stepped towards Tristan, he growled low in his throat. Tristan answered in kind. The hairs on Ashlee's arms stood up in alarm. She didn't want to watch this. Even if it was the best possible thing for Tristan, she couldn't watch her mate get injured and not interfere. Ashlee whirled around to not look at what was about to happen. She covered her ears with her hands and when that was not enough of a separation, she ran for the stairs.

Ashlee called to the gathered people behind her as she ran. "All of you who don't need to be here, come with me, please. We have work to do."

They had to find the witch who'd done this and remove the spell from the shifters so Tristan could be restored to health. And when all of that was done, she was going to string the wretched woman from the roof of the institute. She would leave her out there to rot or freeze, and laugh when the crows got to her.

For a moment, she wondered if she was channeling Tristan's feelings again, but no, they were her own. It seemed when it came to protecting the people she loved, she was a bloodthirsty bitch.

Tristan jerked awake. He snarled and looked around his enclosure with impotent fury. Trapped again. The bars closed in on him for a moment, then he composed himself and walked the length of his five-by-five cell. He knew the measurements because he designed the damn thing. He was Prince Tristan, he would find a way out of this. He pounded on the door.

"Let me out," he bellowed.

The guards always responded to him. They vied for his good favor. One of them was going to help him take care of the pain in his head. He looked down at his hands, they shook violently. He pounded on the door again.

"We're not letting you out, Trip." Rex's voice answered him. They'd been smart, they'd known he could have ordered the guards around. But Rex would never tolerate his demands. It wasn't going to be so easy.

"Rex, please, it will be very fast. I won't even let her suffer. One, two, three, I'll break her neck and then you and I can go to Portland to do whatever it is that you do there." He was being reasonable, despite the throbbing on his front lobe and the needles that poked every inch of his body. Surely, Rex would see that.

"If you could just hear yourself, Trip. You sound just like him. It's horrible." Rex's voice sounded strained.

"Sound like whom? What are you blathering on about, Rexy?" Why couldn't Randolph just be reasonable this one time? Why must he always put up with such a huge amount of incompetence from his family?

"You sound like our fucking father, even your tone of voice has changed. Keep it together, Trip; you have the best thing in the world and she is working like a lunatic to save you."

What? Something about what Rex said stuck Tristan as strange. What was the best thing in the world? He just needed to kill Ashlee and then he would remember, and then the pain would stop. Ashlee…her name brought a pain to his stomach and he doubled over. His love, his life, his mate. He wanted her, needed her to love him.

Obey me.

Oh no.

Kill her.

No.

Obey me, I am your Alpha.

No, Tristan shook his head and fell to his knees. He clutched his head.

Then you will suffer.

The pain started in his feet, a hundred needles attacked him, and then the burning started. He didn't even know when he started screaming, but he was grateful when he lost consciousness again.

Ashlee knew the second Tristan awoke and the second he lost consciousness again. She blinked in frustration and bit her fingernail down to the skin. She was running out of fingernails to destroy.

Michael, Gabriel, Azriel, Theo—who was a little worse for wear after his fight with Tristan—Adeline, Clarinda, Cullen, and five other pack members who Michael called the top 'dominants' who were named, in seated order, Parker, Sean, Jack, Don, and Marlin.

Ashlee blinked again. "Tell me again."

Cullen sighed. Ashlee didn't need to read minds to know he rapidly lost patience with her. "The witch is in the facility with our former Alpha; she is virtually un-obtainable."

"Not true. We just haven't figured out how to get her yet." Ashlee was right and no one would tell her otherwise.

"Say you actually manage to get her out of there, she is a very powerful witch. How do you plan to subdue her?" Cullen's tone started to annoy her.

Ashlee shook her head. "We'll get to that. I want to focus on the getting her out of the building. Tell me about the facility."

"It's a medical building where they bring mental patients. They have doctors, none of the respectable variety, and they use magic to try to build wolf infused super-soldiers and mercenaries that they can control by making Kendrick their Alpha who they are forced to obey. They still haven't been able to duplicate our abilities. Whatever magical forces formed us, it is far above either their scientific or mystical capabilities."

Ashlee stood up. "Do they have a website? How do they promote their shady doctors?"

Azriel grinned and jumped from his chair. "They do have a website." He rushed to the corner of the room and took out a laptop computer Ashlee hadn't noticed was stored there. "I'm the resident computer geek around here. I've been keeping track of their site since it went up about eight years ago." Azriel carried the computer over to Ashlee and she looked down at the screen.

"The Institute for Personal Achievement and Growth. IPAG. He took the name Institute on purpose, because that's what you guys call this place. Located fifteen miles southwest of Playa Del Carmen, Mexico—I've been there on vacation. He's built this practically on top of the Mayan ruins, "Ashlee clicked on the 'contact us' button and moved to the next page of the site. *We at the Institute are always anxious to hear from other medical professionals who might help us build and build our program.* That was how she would get inside the damn building.

"Michael, I need to call home."

Chapter Eight

Tristan's eyes flew open. He sniffed the air and smiled. Rex had abandoned his position by the door and there was someone else watching the outside. *Her*. Had they really been so stupid as to let Ashlee within five feet of him? He would break down the damn door to kill the bitch.

"Hello Ashlee, my love. How nice of you to come and visit with me." He hoped he'd kept the snarl out of his voice, but really, what did it matter? She knew she was dead. Maybe she'd come to accept the inevitable and just finish the whole excruciating process. It would be nice to finally make the burn that accosted his body cease.

"Tristan." He thought he heard a sigh and a sob. Something inside him twisted at the strained sound in her voice. He pushed the feeling down, ignored it. "Rex was right, you don't even sound like yourself anymore." Why did everyone keep saying that? As far as he could tell, he'd never felt more himself, more alive. He was powerful and strong, finally not suppressed by meaningless traditions of morality and falsehoods.

"Blah-blah-blah, darling, smallest violin and all that." Tristan swung his hand in the air in a dismissive gesture, annoyed that there was no one in the room to witness his dramatics. What good did it do to be so fabulous if no one was around to watch him do it?

"Listen to me, Tristan." He heard her fingers scratch at the door. "I know you must still exist, deep down inside, even if it's hidden in the depths of your soul, but I am leaving."

Tristan snarled and he felt his eyes turn wolf. Excellent. He would take great pleasure in tearing out her throat. "There is nowhere you can go, Ashlee, that I will not find you. I will hunt you to the ends of the earth and through time if I have to, you belong to me. You're mine to do with as I will."

"I believe that is true, Tristan. I know you would always find me. You did promise me forever." The sob returned in her voice and he thought he heard her scratch the outside of the door. Why did the sound of this infuriating woman's tears cause his gut to clench like that? Wasn't it enough that he was trapped in this room where invisible bees stung his body every other second? When would he finally have relief?

Kill her.

I am trying, my Alpha.

But he wasn't trying. For some reason, he fought a battle and he didn't know why. Or what the end result would be—even if he won.

"I am going away so I can help you. When I come back, this will all be over. Please believe me."

Oh, he knew she spoke the truth. This would all be over soon, but it wouldn't be because she had gone anywhere.

"Ashlee, if you leave the Institute I will burn it to the ground and kill every person here until you return. Believe *me* because I say that with every fiber in my body, no one here will be safe if you leave." He threw himself against the door that blocked him from Ashlee. A scream of rage tore from his throat when it didn't budge.

"Excuse me, Ashlee."

Whose voice was that? Tristan sniffed the air. Parker, one of the elite dominant guards. What was Parker doing here? The man had no business being near Ashlee. He rushed the door again.

"The Aunts have requested your presence on the observation deck."

Ashlee coughed. Was she getting sick? Why did he care?

He heard Ashlee through the door. "The observation

deck?"

The roof. Why hadn't he ever taken the girl on a tour of the building? Oh well, no time for that now that she was soon to be dead. Too bad, really.

She needs to be eliminated.

I know, my Alpha, I'm working on it.

"I will stay and guard Prince Tristan until one of the other Royals can get here."

Parker still called him Prince Tristan. He would work that to his favor as soon as Ashlee left. Then he'd find her, finish this, stop the pain and get back to things he enjoyed, whatever they might be.

Ashlee stepped through the doors of the observation deck and sucked in her breath. It was an arboretum. Plants of all shapes lined the walls and the ceilings. Exotic flowers with colors she had never seen before, except in dreams, grew to heights above her head. She whirled around in a momentary bliss. The whole room felt peaceful, serene and left a smile on her face.

"Out here, darling girl."

Ashlee walked towards the sound of Clarinda's voice. She walked the entire length of the room until she came out the door on the other side. She stepped through it and onto the roof of the Institute. Clarinda and Adeline stood in the center of a stone circle. Ashlee opened her mouth to ask what they wanted but changed her mind. They would tell her when they were ready. Tristan's soul had given her new insight into the best way to communicate with members of their pack.

Ashlee glanced around at the view that lay out before her. She could see the whole island, the woods followed by the abandoned cottages. The leaves on the trees ranged from purple to orange, and the cold chill told Ashlee the trees would soon lose their colors and become bare in preparation for the winter. Off in the distance, she saw two islands, both appeared uninhabited with no houses or buildings to visible on them. Each island couldn't be more than a mile off the western coast of Westervelt.

"Who owns those two islands?" Ashlee pointed to the land masses, but the Aunts didn't even turn around to look at where she indicated.

"We do, of course. Couldn't have anyone living or working so close to us. It would be dangerous to be discovered."

Adeline beckoned her and Ashlee joined them inside the stone circle. Anxiety soured her stomach. Ashlee didn't know if it was from the upcoming trip to Mexico, or because she stood in a stone circle with two women so mystically powerful, they'd managed to resist the primal urge to follow their mates to death for three decades.

"Sister and I have been discussing this problem of the witch. Truthfully, we thought we had eliminated this spell long ago when we put the wards on the island. We didn't take into account the spell was actually here on the island and not sent into the island from abroad. Your mother could mate your father with no problems because they did not reside here or ever set foot here together. Tristan and you performed the mating ritual here, so Tristan succumbed." Adeline's eyes bore into Ashlee's hard. The older woman cocked her head to the right as if she thought of something she needed to consider.

Ashlee nodded. "So, if I fail at this, then you will need to clear the island. No one can take their mates here. "

Clarinda shook her head. "Not an option, darling girl. Don't you understand? No of course you don't, how could you? We were wrong. Terribly wrong. We assumed Kendrick had the island cursed. We cleaned the land. There is no curse here anymore. There wasn't last night when you mated. No, no, we mistook the spell. It was never on the place. It was on the pack. The people themselves. So when Tristan mated you, he awakened the curse that was all ready on him, laying dormant all these thirty years.

But to leave the island? No, dear. This is our home. We have been here for one hundred years. Before that, the stories say our people ran into trouble at an almost constant pace. This is the first peace we have had for a century, we will not lose it. To remove the spell's presence from the island was not complicated. We checked on it this morning. The others will be safe here with their mates as soon as the spell is removed from Tristan."

Ashlee shook her head. "Why? Why will they all not suffer as Tristan did?"

Her Wolf

Clarinda raised an eyebrow at her. "Because he's very important Ashlee. Or haven't you figured that out yet either? Tristan's fate is hinged to the pack. Where he goes, so does everyone else. We had hoped he would realize it by now. But the boy seems to have invested in self-denial and won't let it go. Perhaps when this is over he will finally see."

Ashlee's head whirled. What they had just told her, it all suddenly made sense. Michael had never fully assumed the role of Alpha. Why hadn't he? Tristan thought he would. But he was wrong. Tristan was Alpha. Oh dear god, Tristan was their Alpha and he was caught in a spell that would not only end his life or hers but everyone's . He was their Alpha and she was his mate.

Only he still had no idea. She'd been resolved to save him from the moment he'd been afflicted but now she knew she'd walk through the fires of hell to bring him back if that was what he needed. She might not have known her wolf for very long but she could feel her in every pore of her body.

Tristan was their Alpha and they would be strong again.

As long as they both didn't perish in tragedy.

Ashlee swallowed hard. "You removed the spell from the island. Can you remove it from Tristan now?" Any chance that this could just end and she wouldn't need to go to Mexico was one she would take.

"No. We're sorry dear." Adeline's voice was so much more serious than Clarinda. "You are not stupid, so I suspect you already know what needs to be done to save Tristan. The witch will have to die, that much you have felt. Then a ritual cleansing spell, a very complicated, powerful undertaking will need to be done on Tristan. Even then it will take magic, strong pack-magic with the whole pack working together to fix him. Clarinda and I never had the chance to save anyone who had succumbed to the spell. Clearing an island is one thing, saving a person already inflicted, that is another matter altogether."

"Can you do a spell that powerful?" Ashlee's question had both the Aunts making twittering noises that must have been laughter.

"Yes, we can. But the spell will have to be done by you, you are his mate." Clarinda explained. "And the bad news is you are nowhere near powerful enough to even attempt the ritual. It would kill you, and then this would all be for naught."

"Even if we had trained you since you were ten, you'd still not be strong enough," Adeline finished.

A sense of dread filled Ashlee. She swallowed it away.

"I will have to be strong enough." There was no other choice. Tristan's face as he'd writhed on the floor in the hall, the look in his eyes when he'd told her to run, all of the images from before his change filled Ashlee's mind. He was hers to honor and protect, she could not fail him. "I have to be."

Adeline smiled. Ashlee took a step backwards from the hardness she saw in a gesture usually saved for happiness or reassurance. "If only it were that simple."

"We can help you," Clarinda, always more gentle than her sister stated. "And we admit that it suits us too. We are tired. But it will be a great burden for you. We are of two minds as to whether you can handle it."

"Handle it?" Ashlee suddenly wanted to be somewhere else immediately. She needed to escape. "Look, my plane leaves in six hours."

"We know that, so we will hurry."

Ashlee heard thunder crackle in the sky. She looked up. It had been clear and beautiful only moments earlier. Lightning struck the ground in front of her and Ashlee leapt back in terror. She turned to run for the door to the arboretum. Instead she hit the ground, hard. Her hands stung beneath her and she turned on all fours to stare at the Aunts. They were both bathed in white light.

Adeline lifted her arms and the light from her body flew from her and into Ashlee. The power hit Ashlee hard and she screamed in agony. The food in her stomach turned over and she retched on the ground.

"Stop!" She begged, pleaded, anything to make the pain stop.

"We're sorry, Ashlee, there is no other way. Be a good girl and take care of Tristan."

Ashlee must have passed out then because she heard nothing else.

Chapter Nine

When Ashlee came to, a fifteen-member band played in her head.

She opened her eyes, but the bright light hurt too much and her hand flew to shield them. Where was she? A little less dazed, she sensed the soft sheets and mattress under her body. She was not on the roof anymore.

"They gave you their power. They're gone now, but they sacrificed themselves so you would be strong enough."

Theo was with her.

HER WOLF

Ashlee squinted at Theo who stood to the left side of her bed. She swallowed. Why did Theo have to be with her when she woke up? She knew, out of everyone, he liked her least. He probably blamed her for Tristan's condition. Truth was, she held herself accountable for it too. If they had just taken the time to even consider the possibility of the spell still being active, they wouldn't be in this predicament now. Her heart panged in her chest. If she lived another hundred years, she would always blame herself for this.

Ashlee pulled herself up into a sitting position. Her head reeled. She didn't want Theo looming over her.

The Aunts were dead?

So that was why they'd behaved so strangely. They'd given her their power, which had ended their lives. A pang of regret pierced through her. Ashlee hadn't even had the chance to tell them goodbye.

Theo cleared his throat. "I don't know if they'd call it a sacrifice. They've wanted to be with their loved ones for a very long time." She touched her head and groaned. "I think they could have found a better method to give me what I needed, or at least a less painful one."

"I'm sorry, perhaps sacrifice wasn't the right word. It was a bit of a shock when the ground started to move and we all heard you scream like you were being murdered. By the time Michael got up to the roof it was too late, they had all but vanished. There was nothing left to hold onto. They just faded away into nothingness. But it's not your fault and I certainly don't blame you."

He didn't? He could have turned himself into the Easter Bunny and she would have been less surprised. Ashlee stared hard at Theo. The usual gruffness and attitude was absent from his face and his posture. He seemed pretty relaxed.

Ashlee's throat felt dry, her voice sounded tight. "I'm sorry they're gone. I only knew them two days, but I liked them very much."

Theo rose and crossed the room to the dresser that held a stainless steel water pitcher. "You know everything they knew. Their powers are yours. I haven't heard of anyone doing that for three hundred years." He handed her the glass he'd filled. "I've been a little hard on you. I was afraid when Tristan met you…afraid of what that meant for the pack. The spell killed everyone thirty years ago but it feels like yesterday to me, and I was afraid that it would all start again. I'm sorry if I turned out to be the Cassandra of the pack. I assure you, it was not my intention, I would rather have been wrong." Theo paused for a second, his brownish, blond eyebrows pointed downwards. Ashlee was struck by how much Theo's insecurity reminded her of Tristan, then she remembered Theo and Tristan had been born only a year apart, so they must have been raised almost as twins.

"You were worried about your brother. I understand." Ashlee smiled. She looked around the room for a clock. What time was it? Had she missed her flight to Cancun?

"You leave in about an hour for the airport." Theo must have read her signals. His eyes lit with admiration before he lowered them in a submissive gesture. "You didn't run. I told you to run when Tristan attacked but you stayed and talked him down, spoke to him and reasoned with him when it should have been impossible. Now you're running off to face our father and his witch. I think you're the bravest woman I've ever met and I'm proud to call you sister."

Ashlee's eyes filled with unexpected tears. She didn't need Tristan's soul to tell her Theo was not a man who expressed emotion easily or trusted others with his feelings. She wasn't going to let any of them down. She would bring Tristan back.

Theo laughed. "Gabriel and Cullen have been arguing all day about who is going with you and your dad to Mexico. They can't agree so they're both going. Michael wants to go too but we won't let him. He's our interim Alpha."

"He needs to do the ceremony." Ashlee knew what the Alpha ceremony entailed, with the Aunts knowledge she felt like she'd witnessed Tristan's father's personally.

Theo nodded. "He will. I believe in him."

"Can you do something for me, Theo?"

Theo nodded, no hesitation, no hedging. He didn't even ask her what she wanted. That was how he treated his family. She felt honored. "Send Rex up to the arboretum, I need herbs. I'm going to disguise my smell so your father doesn't know I'm a wolf. I know how to do that now I'll try to do Gabriel and Cullen too, but he knows them. He doesn't know me.. Then take the ferry to the shore, get in my car, and drive to New Jersey. Go to my mother and demand that she and my sister come here to the island. The spell that I will need to do on Tristan requires one leader and two other mystics. Two other female shifters. The Aunts knew this. They must have known I would need my family. My mother will object, she doesn't want Summer here yet, but there is no choice. If my mother refuses, go and get Summer yourself, or at least threaten to. She goes to Columbia University in New York City. "

"I'll be back with both of them before you return." Theo's eyes held resolve.

"Good, then its time I go witch hunting, don't you think?"

The flight from Portland to Cancun was a blur. Every time Ashlee closed her eyes, she saw Tristan as she'd last seen him, on the floor writhing in pain. Or she heard his voice, so cold and unfeeling, when he'd yelled and threatened her through the door of his cell.

The flight she'd booked stopped in Newark, New Jersey where she picked up her father at their house, and who fortunately remembered her passport. Theo, travelling by car, hadn't yet arrived to pick up her mother and Ashlee decided not to illuminate that fact to her father. He'd be pissed. He didn't like people ordering Victoria around. Ashlee smiled. Scott wasn't a wolf, but she could see now why her mother's wolf had fallen for him.

Daddy. Family. Love. Her wolf stretched out inside of her, content to be with her father even as she worried endlessly about Tristan.

Ashlee stood beside her father outside of the Cancun airport. The heat was not the only thing making her sweat. Cullen and Gabriel had waited inside of the airport, and the plan was for them to follow a few minutes behind, and break through IPAG's security after Ashlee and her father got inside. This would mean they needed to somehow get through the front gate; both Gabriel and Cullen had assured her they were more than capable of handling this, although both had been vague about the details of their plan.

The driver IPAG sent had run to retrieve his car after he informed them that it would take them an hour to get to where they were going.

"You were so quiet on the plane, Ash." It was the first time she and her father had spoken in an hour.

"I'm sorry, Dad. We really appreciate your help with this. You're placing yourself in danger."

"You're my baby, what did you think I would do?" Scott sighed. "When your mother told me she would not outlive me, that she would die when I did, it all seemed very romantic. The first time I saw her wolf, I was awestruck. I never could have become all the things I've become without your mother. She pushed me, in the best possible way. She never let me settle for mediocrity. She has always been my strength, my life."

Ashlee smiled. Her mother knew how to push, even if Ashlee didn't always find it to be 'in the best possible way.' Her father had always been the heart of the family, the gentle one. "Even before I knew you were mates, I found the love you have for each other to be inspirational."

"This boy, Tristan," her father began.

"He's about fifty years older than you are, Dad." Ashlee laughed.

"Regardless, he wants to marry my daughter," his voice sounded rough. "That boy Tristan, if he dies, you die too, right?"

"Now that we are mated, yes. Either that or I'm doomed to live a half-life, never complete, always alone. Never happy." The Aunts had felt that way. She could feel their pain now inside of her. She pushed it down, she didn't need the faces of the men they'd loved haunting her on this trip. She had enough burdens with just Tristan on her mind.

"It doesn't seem so romantic now." Her father grumbled. "And you're sure there's nothing medical science can do to help him? I could load him up on valium, drive him down to Bergen Pines Institute, and let Dr. Lewis have a look at him. He'll come up with a good cocktail of psycho-pharmaceuticals and maybe it'll take care of the problem."

Ashlee laughed, one large blunt hiccup followed. "No, Daddy, but thank you for offering. And he doesn't *want* to marry me. For all intents and purposes, we are married already."

Scott shook his head and pulled his handkerchief out of his pocket to wipe his sweat drenched forehead. "I'm just human, Ash. This man hasn't come to me, hasn't asked my permission, and I haven't walked you down the aisle so, no, you are not married yet."

"Tell you what Daddy, if we get through this and find the witch—which is already unlikely—say we do that, then I somehow subdue her and drag her out of the facility without getting caught, again a big problem. Then we put her in the car, get her back into the United States and onto the boat to the island, where I miraculously perform and survive the cleansing spell, that is after I kill her—"

Her father grimaced.

"Okay, when I let someone else kill her, and save Tristan, then we'll have a traditional human marriage ceremony and you can walk me down the aisle. Deal?"

"Just that little amount of stuff, huh?" Scott grinned at her.

Love him. Her wolf grinned.

Me too. She smiled.

"You look so much like your mother right now." Scott touched her face, on her cheekbone, gently.

The gesture brought tears to her eyes. "People always say that to me, but with my red hair and green eyes, I look like your mother, not mine." Summer looked like their mother. She always had.

"I don't mean your physical looks. Here," He touched her on her jaw line again. "I've loved you your whole life, since the moment you were born. But for the last, I don't know, twelve years, you've seemed so lost. Oh, you pretended to be in love with Tom. Maybe you even did love him a little, but you always seemed hidden, like you weren't complete. Your mother, she has this inner strength, I know it's her wolf. She's unmovable, secure, complete in herself. When I look at you now, we're in the middle of a terribly dangerous time, and yet you seem more *you* than you've ever been before."

Ashlee never got the chance to answer her father as their car pulled up, and the apologetic driver, who couldn't believe how long it'd taken him to get out of the parking lot, hustled them into the car.

Here we go, Ashlee told her wolf.

Good. Tristan.

Yes, we will save Tristan.

―

Tristan knew Ashlee wasn't on the island anymore. Anger surged within him to such an intensity he thought he might explode. Coupled with the sharp needles, the bee-stings, and the burns all over his body—even though he couldn't see the injuries, he knew they were there—now he had to contend with a woman who had disobeyed him. He had told her what would happen if she left. He hadn't been lying.

He sniffed the air. Parker was still outside on guard duty. "Parker, my old friend, what is happening to me?"

Silence met his query for a moment before he heard a chair scrape backwards on the floor. "Prince Tristan?"

"Where is Ashlee? Why am I in this room? Has something terrible happened?" *Believe me*, he silently willed to the guard outside the door.

"Prince Tristan, perhaps I should get your brother."

Bad idea, Michael would see right through his act. "Please, Parker, don't leave me in here."

"You have been struck down by the curse that destroyed our kin thirty years ago. Ashlee has left the island, maybe that's why you're feeling better."

Good. Tristan jumped from foot to foot with excess energy. "Won't you open the door, Parker, so I could get something to eat? I will not leave this room if you like, but I cannot stand to be caged up any longer after my ordeal in the zoo."

"I will open the door for you, Tristan, and then I'll go and get your brothers."

Tristan nodded and tried to put on his most sincere expression for when Parker opened the door. He heard the latch turn on the lock and the door flung open revealing a smiling Parker in front of him. It was a good thing Tristan had earned so much loyalty over the years for being trustworthy and dependable, otherwise he'd never have gotten Parker to open the damn door.

Not wanting to risk his luck, as soon as Parker was fully visible, Tristan leaped on top of him. Being superior in strength and agility, he easily knocked Parker to the ground. But his opponent was a dominant wolf, and an alpha-class at that, so he didn't immediately relent to Tristan's attack.

Parker shoved back at Tristan and soon they rolled

on the ground, each one gaining and then losing position.

Kill him and be done with it.

"But he is not Ashlee. Killing him will not stop the pain, my Alpha."

Parker got a good solid grip on Tristan's neck and pinned him to the floor. Tristan noticed that Parker's eyes had gone wolf. In a moment, he would shift. "Who do you speak to Tristan? Who controls you in this madness?"

"No one controls me, Parker, or you'd already be dead." The burn that plagued Tristan started to creep onto the skin on his neck. Tristan raised his knee and smashed Parker in the groin. It was a low blow, and Tristan knew it, but it stunned Parker long enough for Tristan to regain the upper position in their fight.

Now subdued, Parker groaned in pain. Tristan slammed Parker's head into the wall and his opponent lost consciousness.

"I told Ashlee what was going to happen. She didn't listen, so now this whole place goes up in flames."

Tristan lifted Parker off the ground and swung his body over his shoulder. He wouldn't let him burn to death. After all, there was no sense in wasting a perfectly good hostage

Chapter Ten

Ashlee's first look at The Institute for Personal Achievement and Growth knotted her stomach. She raised her head to stare out the car window as they approached. The building, made of blank tan bricks, looked to be at least fifteen stories high. Two red-brick smokestacks towered above the building and blended into the landscape behind it.

No signs adorned the outside, no indication of what the institutional building was, and no neighbors for miles to hear anyone inside should they scream.

If all had gone according to plan, Gabriel and

Cullen would be twenty minutes behind and ready to break in and out of the facility when she called them by cellphone. Ashlee swallowed her fear; there was no time for anxiety now.

She had a job to do, and a love at home that needed her to do it. Her cell phone rang and she stared at her father in alarm. Michael had given her this phone in case of an emergency. Her father maintained eye contact with her for a moment without speaking as the ring continued. Finally, her Dad nodded to the phone. She looked down at it and answered it.

She gulped. "This is Ashlee."

"It's Az. Michael asked me to phone you. Tristan broke out. He has a hostage and he's going to burn down the place if you don't return immediately. We're doing our best to not let this situation get out of hand, but don't dawdle." Ashlee heard Azriel exhale into the phone.

"I have no intention of wasting time." Don't dawdle? What the hell did they think she had come to Mexico to do, sunbathe? "Tell Michael I've just arrived at the IPAG and I expect him to do everything he can to keep Tristan safe until I get back." She clicked off the phone. Her wolf howled.

Alpha! For now..

Ashlee grimaced. Her wolf was right. Interim or otherwise, everything inside of Ashlee rejected the idea of speaking in any way disrespectfully to Michael. Tristan would hate it. But, the woman she'd been raised to be, despite her breakdown over Tom, would not let her back down. Michael's top duty needed to be to keep Tristan safe until she returned with the witch.

Remorse flooded her system. She picked up the phone and called Azriel back. He picked up on the first ring.

"Ash?"

"I didn't mean to be as rude to Michael as I came across." Her father raised an eyebrow at her. He'd never understand her trepidation and that was fine. Ashlee needed her wolf to settle down before they got out of the car.

Az laughed. "I altered the message you sent slightly when I relayed it to him, sister."

Ashlee smiled. Sister. She was, for all intents and purposes, Tristan's wife, which would make them her family now. "Thanks, Az." She deliberately used his nickname.

"You're welcome."

"Hey, Az, by the way, before I go in, did you ever get to catch that television show the Smurfs?"

"I hate that stupid cat."

Obviously, he'd seen it. "Good luck, Ash." She heard him click off the phone before the sound of the dial tone met her ear. She closed her phone and grinned at her father.

Scott unhooked his seatbelt as the car came to a stop inside the IPAG gates. "Do I want to know?"

Ashlee shook her head. "No. It's pack politics."

"Technically, I am pack."

"You still don't want to know."

Scott nodded. "All right, how long will those herbs you took disguise your wolf smell?"

Ashlee looked at her watch. "Another four hours, which should be more than enough time to either subdue the witch with this," Ashlee pulled a hypodermic needle out of her pocket, which was filled with a combination Nembutal and Phenobarbital, enough of both to knock out an elephant but not kill the witch, "...or get caught by the armed guards and locked in a cell to be experimented on for the rest of my life."

"No one is going to lock you up and experiment on you, sweetheart." Scott raised his shirt to reveal a gun under his sweater.

Ashlee's mouth dropped open. She sucked in her breath. "Where did you get that? Did you have that on the plane?"

"No, Cullen slipped it to me in the airport. He thought perhaps we needed more of an insurance policy."

"Dad, do you even know how to use that thing?"

"I've never used one, but I imagine it's got to be sort of like point and click."

Ashlee shook her head, visions of her father shooting someone, or worse himself, filled her head and she shuddered. "Promise me you won't use it. You have no experience with it and if, God forbid, you actually have to resort to using the gun, then the plan has failed anyway and the best thing you can do is get yourself out and back to Mom."

"You are so focused on saving Tristan. You love him

so much you'd do anything to save him, do you think your mother and I love you any less?"

Ashlee never got the chance to answer, as the door to the car opened and a hand reached inside to help her get out of the car. She took the hand and stepped out. The contrast between the air-conditioned car and the heat of the Mexican desert left Ashlee stunned for a moment. She felt someone grab her shoulders to keep her upright in case she should faint.

Ashlee had no intention of swooning or suffering from heatstroke. She blinked rapidly to clear her head and smiled, hoping to create the image of the dumb, spoiled-brat, her cover persona for the rest of her time in IPAG.

"Daddy," Ashlee spun around to look at her father who had stepped out of the car behind her. "How long is this going to take? I want to go to Señor Frogs tonight." She stomped her right foot. The nightclub had been a favorite of her friends who had spring-breaked in Cancun the year before.

Her father gave her an indulgent look, and Ashlee had to suppress her snicker. If she'd ever really behaved that way, both of her parents would've grounded her. "We will, darling, I promise." He patted her on the back.

Ashlee's father turned to the man in front of her. He held out his hand. "I'm Dr. Scott Morrison and this is my darling daughter, Ashlee." Ashlee felt her shoulders released and she turned to look at the man who shook her father's hand.

"I'm Kendrick Kane. It's a pleasure to have you and young Ashlee here with us, doctor. The Institute has been trying to get a doctor of your caliber interested in helping us develop this place for some time."

Ashlee sucked in her breath and then covered it with a cough. No one had told her how much Tristan resembled his father. He was the spitting image of the man. All of the Kane men resembled each other, and clearly took after Kendrick, but Tristan held the closest similarity. They had the same shade of brownish, blondish hair with an infusion of red. Steady brown eyes shaped just like her mate's stared at Scott as he nodded to something her father said. But Kendrick Kane's eyes were cold, like steel. Even when he was crazed in the hallway, Tristan's eyes had never looked so calculating.

Ashlee pretended to sneeze and inhaled deeply. He didn't smell anything like Tristan either. He smelled unnatural, like hospital sterilization tools and cheap cologne. How could he even stand to smell himself? She would never mistake Kendrick for Tristan, not even in a pitch-black room. She ached for the woodsy smell that Tristan carried and silently she begged the universe to not let her fail at her task so she could be close to Tristan's scent again.

Bad man. He does bad things to his wolf.

Oh yes, bad man. He'd done bad things to his wolf? What did that mean?

Not pack.

No, not pack.

Her Wolf

The basic introductions between Kendrick and her father ended and Ashlee took the opportunity to act up again. "Daddy, I thought you said this was a spa?" Should she stomp her foot again or would it be overkill? Ah, what the hell. She stomped.

"I said it might be a spa, darling, we might help to add a spa to it where my patients can relax and vacation after they've had a little nip or a tuck. They'll also be able to partake of this fine institution's actualization techniques that will help them to become stronger, better people."

Ashlee put her hands on her hips. "Bored, Dad and I don't like to be bored."

Ashlee's father turned to Kendrick. "Is there somewhere my daughter can sit and amuse herself while you show me the facility and we talk?"

"My office has a television and an internet connection."

Ashlee rolled her eyes. "I suppose I could order those new Gucci sandals I've been wanting while I wait for you."

Kendrick extended his arm. "Right this way, Ms. Morrison."

Ashlee's father put his arm around her shoulder and squeezed. "Do you have children Mr. Kane?"

Kendrick shook his head. "No, I don't. I've never been married, never had children."

Evil. I want to bite him and get back to Tristan.

Ashlee shook her head to clear her wolf's thoughts. Ashlee would love to tear him to small, tiny bits and throw away the pieces. But first she had a witch to capture.

Tristan stood back and watched The Institute burn bright orange and red in the distance. Distantly, in the back of his mind, he knew he should feel something about the destruction of a building he'd once designed and helped to build with his bare hands. But, he could barely bring himself to focus on it. He closed his eyes and inhaled the smoke into his lungs. The wood burned first, the insulation would go next. When that happened, it would soak the island in a damp, foul odor they'd never get rid of. Fortunately, it wasn't his problem.

His brothers were near. He could smell them. They kept their distance, and that was smart. The breeze danced on his skin and he smiled at the sensation. It was nice to have even the smallest bit of relief to the constant burn. He looked down at his skin. There was no physical manifestation of his pain, no burns or rash to indicate the trauma that was going on inside of him. If that was odd, Tristan didn't know why.

Kill her, Tristan, kill her.

Love to, but she's not here.

Tired of the constant nagging from his father, Tristan rolled his eyes.

In the distance, he heard a wolf howl. Whose wolf was that? He didn't sound like his pack. The same howl carried through the night to him again. Tristan sucked in his breath. He knew that noise, it was his wolf.

He covered his ears unable to bare the sound. What was wrong with his wolf? The yowl came louder, his wolf was angry. But why? He'd been trying to relieve the pain from them, it wasn't his fault Ashlee hadn't come back yet.

The thought of Ashlee's name brought the wolf shriek louder. Tristan fell to his knees. There was something about Ashlee the wolf didn't like.

Ashlee needs to die.

Mate. We die for our mate, we don't kill her. Or we end our own life and wait for her in the next one, where we beg forgiveness for causing her pain.

His wolf had spoken to him. When had he last heard him? How many hours had it been? Tristan fell even further to the ground, he lay out flat on his stomach, his hands still on his ears to drown out the noise his wolf made.

His wolf was right. Ashlee was his treasure. He held part of her soul inside of his and, needing her desperately, he called to it. She rose up inside of him. Tristan could feel Ashlee's goodness wrap itself around him like a warm blanket. He closed his eyes for a moment but Ashlee roared at him to get up and do something to fix his problem. If he was burning, he needed to put out the fire.

Kill her. That voice, his Alpha

Not Alpha.

Tristan rolled onto his back and screamed. What was happening to him?

You told her you were your mother's son.

He had told Ashlee's mother he was his mother's son. He'd been so sure he wouldn't lose control.

How had he let this happen? He roared, his pain not physical but mental anguish this time.

Kill her

In the back of his mind, he heard Ashlee's soul speak to him again. It wanted him to put out the fire. The cool breeze touched him again and he sighed. Ashlee was right. He needed to cool off, that was the key. But where? The cliffs he stood on gave him perfect view of the water that surrounded the island.

He stood up.

Kill her, boy.

His wolf howled and Tristan ran for the edge of the cliff. The water below would do the trick. He leapt.

In the distance, he heard Michael scream his name as the cool, rough water surrounded him.

If you won't kill her, you will die.
Then kill me.

Chapter Eleven

Ten minutes after her father and Kendrick Kane left her in a pretend snit, Ashlee felt safe enough to start the first part of her plan. In what little time she'd had to prepare for this nightmare, she had tried to be meticulous and organized. She stuck her hand in her pants pocket and felt for the needle that contained her best hope of success. It was still there.

Her wolf wanted blood but Ashlee knew it was wise to be prudent and not just assume that all would be better with the witch's death. They might need the woman. She closed her eyes and let the Aunt's knowledge flow into her. How did someone pick out a witch from say a non-magical person by just looking at them?

Adeline's voice filled her head.

A witch's aura is different from the aura of other people. The magic she carries, it alters her. Close your eyes and let your magic open you to the universe. Once you do, you will see auras and you will see hers is different.

Hell. Why couldn't anything be simple?

A witch will also smell different. She uses many herbs in her potions and spells. Look specifically for valerian, it's foul smelling.

Locating valerian was something Ashlee could actually do. Valerian was also found in potpourri; Ashlee had created some one summer at sleep-away camp. It had soothing properties and when it was mixed with nicer herbs, it picked up the scent of the better smelling plants.

Ashlee opened the door to the office and was relieved to see no one around. It made sense, Kendrick and Claudius wouldn't want her father to know about the non-legitimate aspect of their clinic, they would never be able to explain armed guards or mercenaries hanging around the hallways. In less than four hours, her wolf scent would return so Ashlee needed to hurry.

Lit by fluorescent lights, the hallway outside of the office looked institutional; it reminded Ashlee of the countless hospitals she'd visited when her father dragged her all over the country to see gynecological specialists. She closed her eyes and sniffed. Inside she could feel her wolf become alert. Scents were her wolf's specialty and Ashlee actually looked forward to letting her flex her whiffing abilities.

To the right she smelled nothing, not even the scent of a rodent. She had the sudden urge to turn around and start sniffing at the walls to see if there were any rodents of any kind she could track—for a moment her wolf acted more like a bloodhound. Ashlee remembered the herbs she'd taken to suppress her wolf smell could make her wolf a little loopy. She shook of the feeling and turned her head to the left to sniff in that direction.

Bingo.

All the living and breathing creatures in the building were in that direction. At least it was a place to start. She walked casually down the hallway. She didn't want to seem like she didn't belong there.

She wondered what Tristan would say about this whole arrangement, the inside of this world Kendrick had created. Kendrick ran things here and was treated like an important man, while thirty male wolf shifters waited on an island for someone to explain to them what happened to their world.

In thirty years, they hadn't even done the Alpha ceremony. Technically, the man who created all of this was still their fearless leader. Ashlee's breath hitched as her wolf howled in discontent. Ashlee, herself, was pissed as hell and had to settle for clenching her hands into fists to handle the rage.

She sniffed the air again. She smelled people behind the closed office doors. They were just humans, probably bad ones, but not the witch she needed to find. Herbs, she smelled herbs and they were definitely in the direction she walked. She felt nothing but frustration when she reached the end of the hallway and had not located the witch.

This whole thing would go much better if she could just shift into her wolf form. She pushed that thought away. The last time she'd shifted, she was by herself and would still be there if Tristan hadn't come and rescued her. So she would not attempt the shift here in the middle of this danger zone, by herself, no matter how much her wolf wanted it.

She looked around, the scent was stronger beneath her, which meant the witch was downstairs. Ashlee considered her options, there was an elevator, but she wouldn't have too many escape options if she got caught. Or she had the stairs. The stairs it had to be.

She took the stairs two at time, the clicking of her heels as she ran the only sound as she descended one level.

She pushed at the door. It opened easily, making a loud bang as it hit the wall behind it. Ashlee grimaced at the sound. She scanned the room, worried someone had heard the door slam. But no one was about. She sighed in relief and wondered if everyone was hidden because of her father's visit, or if things at IPAG were always this locked up and quiet.

This hallway was different than the one upstairs. It was darker both in lighting and interior design. The walls were a dark, navy blue color and the lights were not working as perfectly as the ones upstairs. Ashlee guessed they would not be showing her father this portion of the 'hospital' on his 'tour.' She inhaled the air to see what scents she could catch.

The floor she stood on was polluted with scents, one that certainly belonged to a witch. Ashlee smiled; soon this ordeal would be over.

She walked forward, keeping her nose in the air for extra precaution. The longer she used her scenting ability, the easier and broader it became. She caught her father's scent off in the distance, reminiscent of cinnamon and peppermint gum. Kendrick, and his sick wolf smell, was with him. At least she knew he was still okay.

Ashlee passed by a series of one-way glass windows. She gasped and covered her mouth to muffle the sound. Twenty men were visible, although there were parts of the room she could not see. They were strapped down to beds and intravenous lines fed a blue liquid into their arms. The steel straps that secured them to the metal tables were attached at the forehead, shoulder blade, hip, and foot area. Three men dressed in white lab coats paced the room. A woman wearing a long lavender skirt and a black tank top moved around the patients.

Ashlee inhaled the bitter, foul smell of the woman. There she was—her witch. But what was she doing to those men?

Tristan felt himself plummet deeper into the water. He couldn't remember how to swim and that was okay because the cool water was what he wanted on his skin. Chilled and placated by the feeling, he no longer felt the urge to kill Ashlee, nor could he hear his father's voice in his head. He closed his eyes and decided he would stay under the water forever. Somewhere inside of his mind, something stirred to remind him that there was some kind of problem with his plan but he couldn't seem to make out what that was.

Strong arms, four of them, pulled him to towards the surface. He struggled, he didn't want to return to the top, he could just remain where he was. A third set of hands joined the others. Unable to fight off all three of his tormenters, he finally hit the surface. He opened his eyes to see who had captured him and was surprised to see it was Michael, Rex, and Azriel.

Why hadn't they just left him alone?

Michael, holding onto his arms, dragged him onto the beach. "Are you out of your mind? Your woman is in Mexico fighting for your life and you decide to commit suicide now, dooming her to half-life or death?"

Tristan roared. No one was to speak of Ashlee to him. He wanted her dead. "I was not trying to kill myself, the cold water drowns out our father's voice. It makes me want to not kill her. I was just going to stay there permanently."

Azriel, his eyes gone wolf, growled at him. "Has the spell fried all of your brain? You cannot breathe under water, Trip. To stay under water would mean death, you imbecile."

Rex loomed over him. "What do you hear, Trip? Who is controlling you? Who told you to knock out Parker? Why did you burn down our home?"

Tristan snorted. "Our Alpha told me."

Michael glared at him. "I have told you no such thing, Trip."

"You are not my Alpha, brother. You do not want the job. You are nothing."

Rex and Azriel bellowed, the white light forming around them as if they might shift.

"Do I lie, brothers? Could this happen to us with a strong Alpha who controlled and protected his pack? I love our brother, but he is weak, and he has failed us."

Michael's eyes were huge as he stared down at Tristan. "I never wanted this job. I am not meant to be Alpha."

Tristan shook his head. "Then we are all doomed. You should have left me to drown in the water where at least Ashlee would be safe."

Kill her

Tristan shook his head and his brothers stared at him blankly. "I will not."

"To whom do you speak, Trip?" Michael stared at him and Tristan didn't need to read his mind to know that he thought he was crazy.

"My Alpha, my liege, our father."

Tristan watched as Michael turned to Azriel. "Call Gabriel, find out if Ash has the witch yet. I don't think we have much more time."

Kill her.

Tristan closed his eyes as the slow burn started again, and this time when he screamed three sets of eyes stared down at him in horror.

Chapter Twelve

Ashlee needed to get into that room and get the witch out of IPAG before her scent returned and Kendrick could smell her on the premises. The first problem was going to be getting the three men out of the room so she could get to the witch. At least the other men, whatever was happening with them, were strapped down. She had one needle filled with drugs; it had to be saved for the witch.

A plan came to her and she knew right away it was very dangerous. If she got caught she was dead on the spot. She closed her eyes and thought of Tristan, the way his brown eyes shone when he looked at her, and tears filled her eyes. She searched deeper inside of herself and found his soul. He wouldn't want her to do what she was about to try to do. He would have objected to the entire scheme from start to finish. But he needed her and her love for him won over his arguments against doing it.

She knew she was about to run out of time anyway, and her wolf would be better at the fight that was about to come than she would be. She called the shift to her and was surprised at how easily it came this time. Engulfed in a warm, white light, her body painlessly reshaped itself until she was once again a fur-covered wolf.

My turn.

She had to agree, she'd certainly given her wolf leave to control the situation. She looked down at her ripped clothes and picked up the needle she needed to subdue the witch with her mouth. She was particularly careful not to inject herself, the worst things she could do at that very second would be to knock herself out with the damn thing.

I'll be careful.

Good. Her wolf looked around and saw her entrance. The door to the room with the witch was open a miniscule amount, just enough for her nose to nudge open the door. She pushed and walked in. No one seemed to notice her entrance, the three men in labcoats and the witch were consumed with looking at one man who had started to scream.

"Do you think he's going to shift, Mina?" The man to the left of the witch looked at the witch and then back at the man.

Mina, the witch now had a name, nodded. "Maybe. We should unstrap him; the shift is too painful when they're strapped. It killed the last one."

Ashlee's wolf sniffed the air quietly.

Sick wolves in here.

Wolves, where?

Men on table. Very bad things, not normal wolves.

The men on the table were wolves, but not 'normal.' What did that mean?

They make a wolf where no wolf should be.

Oh no. The IVs—whatever was in the IV was turning those men into shifters, sick wolves.

The man to the witch's right scribbled on a clipboard. "How long 'til he launches the assault?"

The witch shrugged. "He wants another twenty soldiers but I think he could take down Westervelt tomorrow with two strong men. Thirty years have passed and they are still demoralized, it'll be nothing to destroy them."

I end her.

No. We need her.

I can't kill her?

No.

Should I get rid of the men with her?

Don't kill them.

The wolf set down the needle on the floor and crouched as she got ready to jump. Her first target was the man on Mina's left, and she leapt on him. He barely had time to yelp before her wolf had thrown him down on the ground and, using her teeth, picked up his head and slammed it onto the ground several times. He lost consciousness within seconds.

She turned and surveyed the room. The man to the right of the witch with the clipboard shrieked and jumped up on an unoccupied metal table.

Silly man.

Using her hind legs, Ashlee's wolf knocked over the table he stood on, he fell backwards to the floor and knocked himself out.

She turned on Mina, whose eyes were huge. She'd backed into the wall. Ashlee called the shift onto herself and embraced the warm white light. The witch opened her mouth but no sound came out. Ashlee knew she was naked and she didn't mind. If it increased Mina's shock, and thereby kept her more defenseless, that was fine by her. She smiled and she hoped she looked as crazed as she felt.

Ashlee cocked her head to the side. "Are you afraid?"

"I, ah—" The witch shook in her shoes and grabbed her throat like Ashlee might rip it out in her human form, too.

"It's very easy, isn't it? To curse my people, to make them slaughter their mates? Not so easy to see me in person." Ashlee walked to the side and picked up the needle she'd dropped. She got really close to Mina, placed her face against the other woman's throat until she could feel her breath in her face. "You took my mate from me, he is rabid right now. I want him back. I'm told you have to die for that and I'm happy to let my Alpha and his brothers kill you, unless you give me a better option." Up so close to the witch, Ashlee could see the wrinkles on her face and the grey that had started to expose itself under her hair dye.

The witch still hadn't uttered a word. "Nothing to say? What did he promise you to get you to do it thirty years ago? Eternal youth? Power? What?" Ashlee jabbed the needle into the woman's neck. Mina sucked in her breath in a little whimper before her eyes rolled to the back of her head and she slumped against the wall.

Ashlee let the woman fall to the floor as she walked quickly to the hall and picked up her cell phone out of her discarded clothing. She dialed Gabriel, it rang once and he answered.

There was no time for niceties. "She's out cold. Are you here?"

"We're here. "

Ashlee sighed. "One big problem we didn't think of."

"What's that, sister?" Gabriel's voice had gone hard, he sounded focused. She suspected he would break down the gate of IPAG to rescue Tristan's mate if he needed to.

"How am I going to get her outside? I'm not strong enough to carry her."

"Wolf-it."

"Wolf-it? You want me to drag her out with my teeth, like she's a freakin' tree branch?"

"Yep."

Ashlee nodded even though Gabriel couldn't see her. "All right."

She called the shift and this time it was harder because she was tired. The white light hit her and she felt herself change. It was still painless but her wolf's first inclination when she appeared was to go to sleep. Ashlee would like nothing more than to find a few more wolves and curl up like puppies for a few hours but there was no time for that. She yawned despite her best intentions to act alert.

A scream sounded from one of the strapped beds. A small sound at first, it turned into a large pain-filled roar. He had started to shift and he was strapped to the table. Ashlee couldn't stand the sight. She trotted to the table and examined the mechanism that held the straps to that bound the man to the table. Once again, she called her shift to become human. All of the shifting around made her feel dizzy. She shook her head to clear the sensation.

She twisted the knobs that controlled the straps that held him down. The straps started to ease up on the man's neck head first. He lifted his head off the table and it twisted from side to side. His eyelids were open but his pupils had rolled to the back of his head so all Ashlee could see were the whites of his eyes.

She twisted as fast as she could, she didn't want him to shift strapped to the table.

Bad wolf.

Ashlee was so focused on her task that for a

moment she did not listen to her wolf. Relief swept through Ashlee as she pulled off the last restraint and the man's screams ceased. In front of her eyes, his body started to twist and contort. There was no white light, no gracefulness about his change. His tongue hung out his mouth, drool streaming from the sides like a slow faucet.

She hurried to release the rest of the restraints, hating the sound of the man's screams. When the last one came off, he rolled over onto his stomach and Ashlee backed up. His bones cracked, his head shook back and forth, and he bucked back and forth on the table. Grey fur appeared on his skin, each new batch seemed to cause the man more and more pain. He rolled onto his back until finally he was quiet.

When he leapt up, he was a large grey wolf and he was mad. He snarled at Ashlee and she took two steps back. He lunged at her and without thought she shifted back into her wolf form.

Bad wolf.

Ashlee couldn't think of anything she had done to warrant this wolf's aggression but she was going to defend herself. She bit at his right ear and growled at him. He drooled and she suddenly worried that he was rabid. She decided not to bite him again.

But how could she fight a wolf that could make her sick? Short answer, she couldn't.

Flee? Her wolf sounded disappointed.

Yes flee, but don't leave the witch.

Ashlee's wolf ran towards Mina and bit down on her

hair. The woman didn't even flinch—her father's drug concoction must have been powerful. Ashlee pulled on her hair and dragged her along the floor behind her. The grey, crazed wolf growled and lunged at her. Letting go of the witch for just a moment, Ashlee knocked over one of the exam tables. It stopped him long enough for Ashlee to take the witch's hair back in her mouth and drag her from the room.

She reached the hallway and using her nose, closed the door behind her. She panted and tried to regain her equilibrium. She sniffed the air, noting that her father and Kendrick had returned to the floor where Kendrick's office was located, where she was supposed to be. Ashlee knew she needed to hurry.

She pulled, as fast as possible, backwards so she could drag the witch's unconscious body behind her. Digging deep for strength she made it up the stairs and towards the front door of the Institute.

"Stop that wolf!"

Damn, someone had seen her. A bullet whizzed by her head, answered immediately by another bullet from behind her. She dropped the witch and swung around to look at who had defended her. Cullen and Gabriel stood behind her, each in their human form, Cullen's gun raised as if he had been the one to shoot. They had exposed themselves to capture for her.

She whimpered in distress at their behavior. That hadn't been the plan, they weren't supposed to let their father know they were around.

Gabriel looked down at her and his smile was so

much like Tristan's she felt actual pain in her chest at the sight. "Like we would let our sister have all the fun here?"

Not what we agreed. It was her first chance to use telepathy with anyone in the pack other than Tristan but it came to her easily.

"I never agreed and neither did Cullen, sorry." At the sound of his name Cullen looked down and grinned too. It was disconcerting to see Cullen smile, she had thought of him as permanently pissed off.

Gabriel reached down and slung Mina over his shoulder. "Cullen, get Scott" With his free hand, Gabriel picked Ashlee's wolf up and swung it over his other shoulder. "We'll be in the car."

Ashlee's wolf groaned. She didn't like to be manhandled by Gabriel and felt she could certainly walk. But if Gabriel heard her complaint, he ignored it.

Ashlee heard five more gunshots behind her and struggled to see what was happening but Gabriel had her tightly in his grip and didn't let her down.

Daddy?

Both she and her wolf were petrified for her father. They got through the front gate and Ashlee looked down to see three dead guards, including the driver who had brought them to the compound, each with their throat ripped out, sprawled on the ground. Ashlee remembered a similar scene from the parking lot outside of the zoo. That time it had been Tristan and Rex who had ripped out their attackers' throats. At least the pack was consistent in their violence.

Gabriel opened his car's trunk and dumped the witch into it before he shut it with a thump. He swung open the back door and slid Ashlee inside.

"I've got him." She heard Cullen say as the backdoor opened again and her father jumped in. Her heart pounded hard in her chest and if she'd been in her human form she might have cried out with the relief she felt at seeing him alive and unharmed. Gabriel and Cullen took their seats up front, Cullen in the driver's seat, and sped down the road.

Her father raised one eyebrow. "Ash?"

It's me, Daddy.

"Do you think you could change back now? I have no problems with your mother like this but seeing you as a wolf is freaking me out."

I don't have any clothes, if I switch back I'll be completely naked.

"Here Ashlee," Gabriel pulled his shirt off and handed it to her father.

Thanks.

She called the shift on herself and this time it was hard. Her bones hurt, head pounded, even her teeth ached. Ashlee didn't know if all the shifters had a hard time shifting back and forth as many times as she had but she'd reached her physical limit. Inside, her wolf snuggled down and went to sleep. Ashlee wished she could do the same. She took the shirt from her father and covered her naked form.

"Glad to see you back." Her father sounded relieved. "How did it go with Kendrick? What happened when the alarm sounded? Where is he now? Did you see Claudius?" The words spit out of her mouth fast and she tried to slow down.

"The man likes to hear himself speak. Whatever else he might be, he is totally committed to his place. He thinks he's going to change the world here. When the alarms went off, he excused himself and left me standing there in the foyer. I tried to look inconspicuous and walk out the front door but I never made it. He must have suspected I was somehow involved because he came back and grabbed me by the arm. I thought for sure I was going to have to use that gun but then Cullen showed up and I think Kendrick looked actually alarmed. He let go of me and ran off. I met Claudius in one of the labs. Kendrick called him his chief medical researcher. But I only saw him briefly."

Ashlee nodded. "He may have already changed the world."

"What do you mean?" Cullen looked at her through the rearview mirror.

"He's made himself an army and they're getting ready to come after us." She really was tired; she looked down and was surprised to see her hands shook.

"Would you say that you shifted more than twice this hour?" Gabriel turned around in the seat so that he stared directly at her, his eyebrows pushed down, a severe look on his face.

"Twice? Try five or six times."

"You're going to crash, sister."

Ashlee opened her mouth to ask Cullen how he

intended to get them over the border to the United States with an unconscious witch in the trunk but she never got the chance as the darkness hit her and she fell asleep.

Tristan looked down at his arms. They were covered in burns and hives. He laughed, the sound choked and raspy. At least his outside matched his delusions now. Under normal circumstances, he could heal himself using meditation but there was no way he could muster that much concentration now.

"Trip?" Tristan turned his head to the sound of the voice. His eyes hurt but he made out Theo's silhouette over by the window. Theo stepped closer to Tristan. "Are you in a lot of pain, Trip?"

Tristan choked. "Yes."

"Victoria is here with Ashlee's sister, Summer. They're outside the door. Michael says Gabriel, Cullen, Ashlee, and her father are on their way back. They're an hour away, maybe less. When they get here we'll start the ceremony and you'll be better."

Tristan blew out his breath. Theo was actually trying to be comforting. He must really be dying. "I don't know, little brother, I'm not sure I'll still be here in an hour. I feel like I'm going somewhere, fading."

"No one has ever hung on as long as you have. You were afflicted three days ago, you're still here, and so is Ashlee. You'll make it, so will she."

Kill her, it will cease.

"When you say her name it becomes difficult for me to resist the urges I'm focused on keeping at bay."

Theo nodded. "Sorry."

"It's okay, I'm going to do my best to make it through this but you must promise me something. You won't let me kill her. You'll kill me, instead. I know we're both doomed, but I can't be the cause of it. Ashlee's light can't be snuffed out because of me. I can't go off into the next life like that."

Theo looked solemn. "I promise. I won't let you hurt her."

Maybe they'd all get through this, but Tristan wouldn't place money on it. At least he'd gotten to be with Ashlee that one night, it was more than he ever imagined.

Chapter Thirteen

Ashlee stood in the center of the sacred circle she'd just created. One hundred gray rocks, each placed exactly five inches from the one next to it. The Aunts had never done this spell to save any of the men from the pack. When they'd first been bespelled, there hadn't been time. Everyone had been dead before there was time to even reflect on what happened. That left Ashlee with the unfortunate circumstance of not being one hundred percent certain that what she was about to undergo would even work.

Her mother and Summer stood on the other side of

the rocks, each with pensive expressions on their face. Their mother looked worried, concern raged on her features and Ashlee didn't have to read minds to know Victoria's nerves were shot. If this didn't go well, her oldest daughter would be committing ritual suicide by the end of the night.

Summer looked confused, but as was typical with her sister, she still held a defiant glimmer in her eyes. She'd only just found out about the half-wolf shifter part of their heritage. In typical Summer fashion, she was just a teensy bit skeptical.

Summer crossed her arms over her chest. "Ashlee, you can't really be serious."

Ashlee sighed. Her sister had asked her the same question ten times already. "I'm totally serious, Summer."

"You're really contemplating killing yourself over some guy?"

"He's not just some guy, Summer. He's my mate and that makes him the equivalent of my husband, maybe even more powerful than that, and someday you will understand." Ashlee pushed the hair off her forehead; she'd been covered in sweat for hours.

"And seriously, you can't really expect me to believe that I'm suddenly going to start turning into a wolf."

Summer, her baby sister, had always been the more skeptical of the two of them. Blonde haired and blue eyed, she looked like a miniature clone of their statuesque mother. If not for the height difference between mother and daughter—Summer stood five feet tall—Ashlee always felt it would be hard to tell Victoria and Summer apart. The only other difference was that Summer had worn glasses since childhood and their mother had never needed them.

Ashlee grinned a knowing smile at her mother. "Mom, would you mind? I need to reserve all of my energy for the spell."

Her mother nodded and called the shift onto herself. Summer shrieked and took two steps backwards as her mother became a white wolf.

Ashlee cocked her head to the side. "Still don't believe?"

"And you can do that?" Summer's voice shook.

"Yes."

Ashlee watched as Summer approached their mother, slowly. "And I'm going to do that?"

"Maybe."

Ashlee looked back at her circle of stones. She had her two female shifters, her circle of rocks and her understanding of how things were supposed to go in the spell. Which meant she just needed the pack and Tristan. They should all be arriving momentarily. Michael had warned her that they would be bringing Tristan out in chains to keep him from hurting either himself or her.

Ashlee's mother called the shift back onto herself and stood before them naked. Summer closed her eyes and turned around. Ashlee grinned and wondered suddenly if it had only been a week since she'd met Tristan and had the same reaction to her mother's nude form?

A sharp pain hit her abdomen and she doubled over onto the ground. Her mother quickly stepped over the stones and grabbed her shoulders as she pulled her into a sitting position.

"What is it, Ash?"

"Pain in my abdomen." It passed, but she still felt shaken. She didn't know what it was and the last thing Ashlee needed was anything else to distract her.

Voices in the distance alerted Ashlee that the pack's arrival was imminent. She stood up and brushed herself off, by the end of the ceremony she'd most likely be naked, but she wanted to start out looking presentable.

Ashlee's mom still had a worried look on her face, not wanting her mother to obsess about pain they couldn't investigate at the current time, she changed the subject. "You left Dad where?"

"In one of the abandoned cabins. I can't believe Tristan burned down the Institute."

"When this is over, he's going to beat himself up about it." It was important to sound confidant, Ashlee reminded herself. She reached down deep inside to touch her beloved's soul. His love flung outwards to her and she closed her eyes and smiled. When this was over, she would never be separated from him for any length of time again.

Her eyes suddenly fell on the chained form of Tristan. Azriel and Theo led him up the hill. Michael walked a pace behind them, Rex to the left of the group. Tristan raised his eyes to look at her and she sucked in her breath. His pupils were huge, the whites bloodshot. What she could see of the skin on his arms and legs, he looked burned. He'd really been through hell while she'd been gone.

She fought back the urge to rush to him, throw off his chains, and embrace him with so much love it healed his wounds. There would be time for all of that after she succeeded in removing the spell from him. There had to be.

Tristan fought his chains, causing Ashlee's heart to lurch. One way or another his pain would end today, she would see to that. She would either remove the spell or give her life for him. Either way, it would be her gift to him.

"Listen up." She kept her voice authoritative, she was the only person here who could conduct this ceremony and everyone was going to abide by her rules. "Once I have started the ceremony. No one, and I mean no one, is to cross the rock barrier. It could harm you. I'm going to be calling on the communal magic of the pack to assist me towards the end of the spell. You may feel strange when I do that, but don't worry, you're perfectly safe." Ashlee paused and swallowed her fear.

You will be fine

Ashlee was glad for her wolf's vote of confidence and she took a deep breath. "Theo, please put Tristan in the center of the circle and take the chains off of him.

Tristan growled and tugged on his chains as he tried to get to her. Theo stared at Tristan and then back at Ashlee. "I don't know if that's such a good idea, sister."

Ashlee shook her head and clenched her teeth. She would not compromise the legitimacy of the spell. Those chains were made of metal; they might alter the purity of the stone-circle. "He has to be unchained for this to work, Theo."

Michael interrupted Theo's argument with Ashlee. "As you say, Ashlee." Theo brought Tristan to the center of the circle and took off his chains. When the chains came off, Tristan fell to the ground and stayed there for a moment before he sat up and glared at Ashlee.

"This isn't safe for you, little one." He growled. "I thought I told you to run."

"And so I did, Tristan." Ashlee looked out of the circle to Michael. "Is it done?"

Ashlee needed to know if they had disposed of the witch. Before that very moment, Ashlee would have thought the idea that someone she associated with had killed another person would make her feel repulsed but she felt just the opposite about it. They needed Mina dead—her blood was part of the ceremony and besides, the woman had signed her own death warrant thirty years earlier when she'd maliciously cursed the wolf-shifters. Ashlee had watched her mother, Rex, and Tristan dispose of the would-be kidnappers outside of the zoo without many mental ramifications. Evidently, she was stronger than she'd given herself credit for.

"Cullen completes it now. You don't need it until the end of the ceremony, yes?"

Ashlee sighed; she really would have preferred to have had it now. But the sun was right in the sky so she'd have to count on Cullen to show up with the blood.

"As long as I have it by the end. Actually, it's not a bad idea for you all to know this in case I am not able to do it myself—pour the witch's blood in the center of the circle. It will finalize the spell and call off the magic."

"Ashlee," Michael stared at the ground. "I'm not the Alpha. Not really."

Ashlee nodded. "I know who the Alpha is."

"Do you think I have enough power without the Aunts to handle this?"

"You'd better." She couldn't be any more assuring than that. Truthfully, Ashlee had no idea what would happen if they failed.

Ashlee closed her eyes to prepare for her task. She wished she could have practiced this once before she had to perform it in front of the entire pack. Tristan made a groaning noise and she opened her eyes, she could see he struggled and she knew that she was running out of time.

The first thing Ashlee needed to do was invoke protection on her stone circle. She raised her left hand towards the setting sun in the sky.

"I call upon thee, Watchtower of the East. Protect this circle and those who surround it. I call upon you for sanctity against those who would cause us harm."

The breeze picked up and bounced through Ashlee's hair. The skirt she wore fluttered around her ankles. Ashlee smiled, she felt powerful and capable.

Her Wolf

Keep going. Keep focus

Ashlee might be new at mysticism but her wolf acted like she was an old expert.

"I call upon thee, Watchtower of the South. Protect this circle and those who surround it. I call upon you for sanctity against those who cause us harm."

Lightning struck in the sky followed immediately by a loud boom of thunder. Ashlee raised her eyes to look at the clouds. They swirled above their heads, counterclockwise. She'd gotten someone's attention.

"I call upon thee, Watchtower of the West. Protect this circle and those who surround it. I call upon you for sanctity against those who cause us harm."

Inside the circle, rain started to pour on Ashlee and Tristan but Ashlee could see that the others remained dry. Her mother called out something to her but Ashlee couldn't hear it over the wind and the rain, she could see her mother's mouth moved, but the words just sounded like nonsense. She turned to stare back at Tristan who had stood up. He seemed glued to the ground on the other side of the circle, his hand in fists.

"Ashlee, what are you doing? You cannot win this. It's too late for me. Run, while you still can." His voice sounded desperate. "Find a spell that separates us, that undoes our mating. Then you'll be safe. Leave me."

Ashlee's eyes welled up with tears and the little control she possessed on her emotion was lost. "Leave you? Out of everything you have said to me since you woke up bespelled, that is the worst. I can't leave you, I never will. I'm carrying a piece of your soul around inside of me, just as you have mine. Neither of us will ever be okay without the other one. If one of us dies, the other does too. Get over your macho ideas. I'm in this for the long haul.

The wind sped its assault on her face and she raised her arm to block its way. Tristan stood still, his breaths coming in sharp pants. His fists clenched at his sides he roared loudly before he spoke. "I will not have you hurt, Ashlee. I can't be the cause of that, either by my own doing or because you are hurt trying to help me."

Ashlee knew she would feel the same if the situation was reversed. But she couldn't focus on that now. If she were cursed, Tristan would move heaven and hell to save her. She would do no less for the man whose very existence had altered her life so completely.

"I call upon thee, Watchtower of the North. Protect this circle and those who surround it. I call upon you for sanctity against those who cause us harm."

From out of the gray rocks, Ashlee had laid on the ground, steam rose to the sky. It encircled Tristan and Ashlee until she could only see only him. It was like they were the only two people left on earth.

Ashlee swallowed so her voice wouldn't shake "Well, Tristan, one way or another, this spell will cease to plague us, my love."

"Ashlee, I don't think you appreciate the tenuous hold I have on my control. "

Tristan sounded desperate and Ashlee hated it. Soon he would be the man who fate had chosen for her to mate, who had ordered her to free him from the cage and rescued her when she'd been alone in the woods. If Ashlee had her way, Tristan would never again have to suffer like this.

Ashlee leaned back and raised both arms to embrace the sky. The rain pounded down on her, it was cold. She closed her eyes and ran through her depth of knowledge one more time. What the Aunts had known, she knew. It would have to be enough.

When she opened her eyes, she felt calm and sure of herself, clear in her resolve.

"I call upon the fates that created us, the power of magic that runs through our veins, the spirit that guards all animals. I ask you for the power to see." Ashlee felt a little bit dizzy but she would not fall down. "I plead with you for the power of sight so that I might save him." Ashlee fell forward, overwhelmed by the surge that hit her body.

She felt like she'd fallen twenty stories. Somehow she found the strength to stand back up. When she looked at Tristan, she knew she succeeded in her task. She could see the spell all over him.

Tristan stood, still tall and proud despite his slumped shoulders. His face, an unreadable mask of emotion, looked exhausted. But now Ashlee could see the spell the witch had cast so many years ago like it was a living, breathing entity on Tristan. It fed on Tristan, behaved like a parasite, ate at his very soul while it injected itself into his bloodstream. The damn thing was toxic and if she didn't get it out and off of Tristan, it would kill her mate.

Ashlee could see the spell. It covered Tristan's whole body. Lines formed and disappeared as it moved over him and ate away at his soul. The malignant spell had a sickly green hue and Ashlee couldn't help but be reminded of the way vines eventually strangled the trees they lived on to death. That was what was happening to Tristan. But now she could see it and now she would destroy it.

Chapter Fourteen

Ashlee flung her hands towards the sky. It was time to lower the separation between Tristan and the others. Pack magic was all that could help them now. She needed to call upon the magic they jointly shared—the special gifts that allowed them to shift and to speak with each other telepathically. Essentially, Ashlee was going to borrow the magic of her kin and pour it into Tristan until he was clean of the spell. Then they would finish it off by pouring the blood of the witch—she hoped Cullen had finished with the witch by now—on the ground of the sacred circle which would cleanse the island and prevent other witches from performing spells to curse them.

Piece of cake.

If only she shared her four-legged counterpart's confidence. If the aunt's knowledge was to be trusted, calling down the elements for protection and being gifted with the sight was the easy part. This next part might be tricky.

"Barriers down." On her command, the fog that had surrounded them lifted skywards. The pack once again surrounded her.

Her voice sounded secure and that was the best she could do. Tristan's eyes turned wolf and she hoped he wasn't going to call a shift onto himself. This Tristan she could work with, as a wolf she might as well lay down and let him kill her.

She took a deep breath and reminded herself that when this was over, she would have her Tristan back. The man who had promised her a future she'd actually believed in, who didn't care that she couldn't conceive babies, and who had been willing to leave everything he'd ever known or loved to be with her. He was an extraordinary person whose soul she held with her own. In the end, this would all be a memory, and their future would be what counted.

For the last time, Ashlee raised her hands as she stared at Michael. This would all come from him, the Alpha. His power was their own. "I call upon the powers that made us to fill me with our pack magic so I may cure Tristan of this malicious spell and free the pack of this burden." The words, formal and remote, weren't her own, but they flowed off of her tongue like she had said them for years.

Ashlee looked out of the circle to the pack. The spell would call on them now. Michael fell to his knees. He screamed in agony and a red light pushed out of his body into hers. Ashlee braced herself for the power to enter her but the surge that found its way into her body was light and easy for her to handle. She frowned. She certainly didn't feel more powerful but maybe that was how it was supposed to work.

Tristan grabbed his head and fell to the ground and did not utter a sound. Ashlee could see the spell that was woven around Tristan start to pulsate, as if it understood she was going to rid Tristan of its impurity. Even in her panic for her beloved, Ashlee couldn't help but think that the witch who designed it had been particularly devious. At the first sign of its removal, it had been set to kill the victim. Well, she would be faster.

She pooled what little pack magic she had received through her body and raised her hand, willing the power to travel through her body, into her hand, and out toward Tristan. Then, if she was lucky, she would be able to direct the power over Tristan's body where the spell ate at him.

Ashlee pushed the power from her body. It exited without too much fuss and Ashlee wondered where the excruciating pain the aunts had thought would accompany the power transfer was. Tristan's body absorbed the power and Ashlee thought she heard some gasps from the pack that stood in silence around her circle of stones.

The spell, a brownish, green color on Tristan's body waned, a little. Ashlee saw Tristan take a deep breath, relief evident on his beautiful features. He looked up at her from the ground where he lay and opened his mouth to say something. With a wrenched groan, he rolled over, pain once again obvious on his face.

Ashlee shook her hand hard. Where was the power? The power was all gone, she'd passed all of it onto Tristan and it still hadn't been enough. In front of Ashlee's eyes, stars appeared. She shook her head to try to clear the sensation but it didn't help. The sensation increased until she had no choice but to sink to her knees to try to clear the dizziness.

Don't feel well.

What did it mean that her wolf felt ill? The aunts knowledge rushed into her head. She closed her eyes first against the surge and then to block out what the aunts had known about the ritual failing. Ashlee hadn't accessed this particular data earlier, or maybe she hadn't wanted to know, which she silently admitted was more likely the case. The truth was that once a shifter invoked the powers that created them, the only outcomes were success in the spell, or death by it.

Ashlee failed to save Tristan. She hadn't been powerful enough, and now she would die. She looked down at her hands. They shook violently. Tears welled up in her eyes at the unfairness of this outcome. Fate had brought them together to separate them so soon? Would death this way be painful? She wished she could reach out and grab Tristan, feel his arms around her as she faded away. Ashlee closed her eyes to touch Tristan's soul. It was still there, still intact. He wouldn't blame her for what happened, she could feel that in that part of him that she carried.

Somewhere in the distance she heard voices raised in alarm, one of them was distinctly Tristan's, the other her mother. Ashlee couldn't be sure but she thought she might have heard her sister yelling too. She raised her head to try to look at all of them, but everything was a blur.

She closed her eyes. What happened to the person who failed at the spell? Did they get to meet their mate in the next life or was it eternal suffering? Ashlee hit the ground hard, unable even to muster the strength needed to break her fall. The dirt felt cool. It soothed her until blackness surrounded her every thought.

Tristan watched in horror as Ashlee hit the ground. Whatever she'd done, it had cleared his head and for however long that lasted, he wasn't going to waste time. Inside, his wolf howled in alarm, desperate for the shift, dying to save his mate. Agony marred the muscles straining to change the form of his muscular body, as his mind fought to keep the inner beast caged. Tristan held him back, there was nothing his wolf could do right now.

He turned to the pack that stood in horror around the sacred circle. Looks of terror showed on their faces. Ashlee's mother wept, held up by a young woman who looked so much like Victoria, Tristan had to assume it was Ashlee's younger sister.

He ran to the edge of the circle, directly in front of Victoria, cognizant of the fact that he couldn't cross the stones without risking danger to everyone. "What was she trying to do?"

Victoria sniffed. "She called on the pack magic to clear you of your spell but it must not have worked."

Tristan felt slightly better, but yes, Victoria was right, he wasn't clean. He could feel the madness, like worms crawling all over his body, start to take hold of his consciousness again.

Tristan shook his head. "Why didn't it work?" His heart pounded in his chest, he wanted to run to Ashlee, to scoop her up in his arms, but if the spell resurfaced he couldn't trust himself to be close to her.

Michael cleared his throat. "The pack is weak. Their magic, our magic, isn't strong enough for what she needed." His brother's face was raw, his voice strained. This was going to eat Michael up alive.

Tristan stared at Michael. His brother was a good man; he had trained as a warrior, and his wolf was strong but he was a terrible leader. He hadn't been the first of their brothers to stand up against their father. Instead he had hoped for a peaceful outcome. As it was, he still couldn't decide on a course of action to attack IPAG. He didn't have the stomach for the Alpha job;

Her Wolf

he would do better as an advisor.

They'd all been trying to tell him. But he hadn't listened. It seemed so clear now.

Tristan knew what he had to do, and he knew he didn't have much time to get to it done.

He stepped to the center of the circle. "I am Alpha of this pack." His voice sounded strong, and inside of him his wolf howled in delight. Yes, this felt right. The pack needed a strong leader and it was him. He'd survived months in a wolf cage and managed to hold off the spell of a witch that had ended the lives of countless others. Ashlee made him strong. He could endure anything. For her, he would lead the pack in the direction it needed to go.

"Who would challenge me?" Tristan, like every trained member of the Westervelt pack, knew there needed to be a challenge to solidify the claim of leadership. The Alpha ritual required a challenge. Tristan looked around the group and awaited the announcement of his opponent, fully expecting Michael to step forth. His eldest brother cleared his throat and opened his mouth. Tristan cringed. He didn't want to fight Michael. In the past, the challenger frequently died as the Alpha fury overtook the two opponents. Michael never got the chance to continue.

From behind the group, Cullen stepped forward. "I challenge you." The most feared shifter alive, the oldest of them all, his father's enforcer stepped forward. Tristan watched as Cullen handed a cup full of liquid to Theo and then crossed the stones to enter the circle. Down the side of Cullen's face were five bloody scratches that looked to have been made by someone's nails as they'd dug into Cullen's skin.

Tristan had a moment to register that the rocks had let him pass unharmed. He was the rightful challenger. Cullen could never be Alpha, not even if he beat Tristan in this fight. His blood was not royal. It did not hold enough magic. There was only one reason Cullen would undertake a battle he couldn't win—he wanted to lose. Oh, Tristan knew Cullen would fight until he had no breath left in him, he wouldn't let Tristan beat him on purpose. But if Tristan won, and he intended to, this would be Cullen's out, his ritual suicide without the ritual. Tristan could respect that he wanted to die this way. It was a warriors' out.

The blood inside of Tristan started to heat. It only took a moment. Tristan could feel the shift and play of his muscles and bones shifting beneath his heated skin. The beast growling in its delight to fight. He was ready to fight Cullen to the death, bloody though it would be, Cullen craved death. Cullen would have the death he desired and deserved as the warrior he was.

"Mother, what's happening?" Ashlee's sister called out in fear and Tristan heard Victoria soothe her.

"It's the Alpha challenge, Summer, it will be okay. Tristan's going to save Ashlee. He's going to save us all."

Cullen's head whipped to the side, his eyes wide, shocked. Tristan followed his gaze as he stared at Summer. Recognition hit Tristan hard—Cullen Murphy had just found his mate and it was Ashlee's sister. Tristan remembered the crazed feeling well, the insanity that held him for a moment when he'd realized he'd finally met his other half, the peacefulness that had immediately followed that knowledge.

In any other circumstance, he might have let Cullen out of the challenge, but not today, not while Ashlee lay dying. She was his first priority. Only by performing the challenge could he claim the Alpha position, and thereby save Ashlee with the pack's true magical force. His only chance was get Cullen to back down.

Tristan called the shift onto himself and leapt onto Cullen, who was still in his human form. His wolf howled. He didn't like Cullen still so weak, so distracted. Cullen shifted faster than Tristan had ever seen done before and snarled at Tristan as he flung Tristan's wolf from his body. Cullen's wolf was gigantic. He stood heads over the others and dwarfed Tristan whose wolf was certainly not small. Tristan stared at Cullen's brown wolf and felt the Alpha fury fill him. He was Alpha and this underling had dared challenge him.

Tristan bared his teeth. He would tear Cullen limb from limb. Tristan leapt in the air and landed on Cullen's back. His teeth bit into Cullen's fur. Furious, he tore and bit into the dark brown wolf. He was Alpha, he would be obeyed.

"Mom, please don't let Tristan kill that wolf."

Summer's voice hit Tristan hard. It passed through his Alpha fury into his consciousness. Her voice was so much like Ashlee's.

"There's nothing I can do, baby."

Victoria let out a sob. Tristan realized she knew exactly what was happening. If he wasn't careful, Ashlee's mate would kill Summer's.

Cullen, freeing himself momentarily from Tristan's assault, bit hard on Tristan's side. He backed up, showing his teeth in fury. Tristan didn't know if Cullen could still be reasoned with or if he was gone to the anger that accompanied the Alpha fight.

Yield to me, Cullen.

Cullen snarled. *Never.*

I will be Alpha and you will be dead. Who will care for your mate? She has never known you, will never have a mating ritual. Neither of you will ever know the joy of that.

Tristan leaned back on his back legs, ready to pounce if Cullen did not yield.

She is mine?

Only you know the answer to that.

You think to trick me, to distract me from this fight.

Tristan snorted through his snout. *I am stronger than you; I could kill you any time I pleased. Instead, I tell you to yield so that you may know your mate.*

I have waited a long time. I hardly believe it.

Do you yield?

Cullen paused for a moment and Tristan could see a war of emotions rage in his wolf eyes.

Cullen dropped to the ground, his eyes lowered, his body in a submissive stance. *I yield, my Alpha.*

Moving with instinct alone, Tristan called the shift back onto himself. He stood before the pack. Sweat dripped from his muscles, his breath coming in short gasp as his human form gained control

Kill her. She's almost dead anyway. He heard his father's sick voice in his head, but it was weak, he could barely make out the words. It was time to complete the cycle and end the spell. He looked at Ashlee, unconscious on the ground and he raged inside.

He spoke the words the Alpha shifters had spoken since the beginning, they poured out of him as if he'd always been meant to say them. "I am your Alpha, I am your liege. You owe me your fidelity. I will have your power now."

Around the circle, compelled by magic and Tristan's force of will, each member of his pack fell to their knees. A red light pushed out of each shifter, causing each of them to shift to their wolf form before the lights slammed into Tristan. He fell to his knees and closed his eyes.

He heard Summer scream as it was her turn, her first shift upon her but he couldn't watch. Each beam of red was part of his pack member's soul. It belonged to him now, it was his to safeguard. The responsibility overwhelmed him.

Inside of him, his wolf paced back and forth and roared with delight. It had been waiting for this day, had always known it was Alpha.

Tristan tried not to smile. *Why didn't you tell me? Not for me to tell.*

The Alpha power drove the spell from his body. Tristan opened his eyes. On top of his skin, his burned flesh disappeared, replaced by new skin. His eyes smoldered and tears fell down the sides of his face. He closed them and when they reopened, seemingly of their volition, the world looked different to him.

I see out of them now too.

His eyes had gone wolf; they would stay that way now forever, as his father's had been before he betrayed them. Tristan would not follow the same path.

A wolf rubbed against him, he looked down, it was white and red—Ashlee. He stroked her with his hand, rubbed her head and finally pulled her small wolf body into his arms.

The spell's not totally gone yet, my Alpha

He flinched at the word used by Ashlee. That is not what she would call him but this was not the place to argue or the time for it.

It's not? I feel cleaned.

Ashlee called the shift onto herself and she glowed in the white light as it surrounded her. Tristan sucked in his breath; she had done that so easily. The spell had caused him to miss Ashlee's transformation into a secure, magically talented wolf. He would see his father dead for that alone.

She approached the side of the circle and picked up the cup filled with red blood that Cullen had brought. Walking to the center of the circle, her legs shook as if she wasn't steady. He stood up to help her and she smiled weakly at him.

"You called me back from death. I heard your Alpha yell and I needed to give you my allegiance." She touched the side of his face with her free hand. "You already had my love." Ashlee poured the red liquid onto the ground in front of them. "Now you're clean." With that last sentence, she collapsed in his arms.

Chapter Fifteen

Ashlee looked around the abyss she'd awoken to and tried to make sense of what she could remember. She failed in her attempt to remove the spell but Tristan had done the Alpha ceremony and become the leader of their pack, freeing himself from his father's curse.

"I've been waiting to meet you for so long." Ashlee whirled around. In front of her stood a woman who looked to be twenty years old with chestnut brown hair and grey eyes. She grinned from ear to ear and she wore a long, floor length white dress.

Ashlee swallowed. "Am I dead?"

Her Wolf

The woman laughed. "No, you passed out and I brought you here for a few moments, although I'm giving my son a bit of a heart attack at the moment."

"Your son?" Realization dawned on Ashlee. "You're Mary Jo? Tristan's mother?"

Mary Jo nodded. "And you're Ashlee, Tristan's mate. I wish I could have lived to meet the children you will have."

Ashlee opened her mouth to tell Mary Jo she wouldn't be having any babies but before she could Mary Jo placed her hand on her belly.

"You can now."

"What?" Ashlee was confused.

"The pain in your abdomen that keeps coming and going, it's your wolf healing your reproductive organs. She's fixed what was wrong."

Tears welled up in Ashlee's eyes. Babies? She could someday have children with Tristan? She swallowed hard and Mary Jo pulled her into her embrace. She stood like that for a moment, feeling content to let Tristan's mother comfort her. Finally, when she felt foolish, she pulled back and wiped her eyes.

"What is this place?"

Ashlee watched Mary Jo glance around the room. "It's where we wait for our mate to join us so we can go to the afterlife together. It was very crowded for a while, when I first moved on, a few days ago my sisters-in-law finally met up with their husbands who had been waiting here with me. Now it's quiet."

Ashlee narrowed her eyes at Mary Jo. "You're still

waiting for Kendrick? Why would you do that after what he's done?"

Mary Jo sighed. "He's my mate, and whatever has happened to him to make him as sick as he is, to make him do the things he's done, I will always love him, even if I can't forgive him or even begin to understand."

"So, it's been lovely meeting you, really it has. You raised six wonderful men, and of course I'm rather fond of one in particular. But if I'm not dead, why am I here?" Ashlee wanted to get back to Tristan. He was finally healed and she needed to see him.

"I want to tell you how to bring the women back."

Ashlee grinned. "So, it's safe then, from the curse? We can bring the other women back."

Mary Jo nodded. "Yes, the shifters will no longer try to kill their mates. You removed the curse when you spilled the witches' blood and Tristan is strong, his magical connection to the pack will keep others from being able to do what the witch did."

Mary Jo approached Ashlee and placed her hands on her shoulders. "But the danger isn't done, darling. It's just beginning. The men will need their women in the battles that will come. I don't know how Kendrick can be stopped. If I did I would have stopped him thrity years ago. But I do know it will be mated couples who will be our salvation."

"How do we find the women to bring them back?"

Mary Jo leaned over and kissed Ashlee on her cheek. Electricity shot through Ashlee's body and her head pounded. She almost fell down but Mary Jo held her up.

"Now you know what I know." She kissed her other cheek. "Good luck."

Tristan saw Ashlee's head move back and forth on the pillow and he took a deep breath of relief. She'd been so still, almost not breathing and it had terrified him. He wasn't even clear why she'd been unconscious for twelve hours when physically she seemed so perfectly well.

"Ashlee, are you coming back?" He kneeled down next to the bed and stroked the hair off her forehead. He'd almost lost his precious gift. Silently, he promised himself he would never again come so close to losing her.

Her eyes still closed, she whispered, "I'm so sick of these women doing that to me."

Women? "What are you talking about, little one?"

Ashlee opened her eyes and stared into his. His heart dropped into his stomach and he felt joy surge through his system. She was awake, and even if she wasn't making any coherent sense, she talked. Ashlee threw her arms around him and squeezed him tight against her. He wrapped his arms around her as his body shook with unexpressed emotion and finally fear within him released.

She pulled back to speak. Her voice shook. He touched her face, gently stroking her features as he lowered her on the bed, sure that she must be still weak.

"The women in your family keeping knocking me on my ass to deliver knowledge to my brain. One of these days, I'm going to short circuit and then what good will I be? Answer me that." Ashlee tried to sit up again and Tristan leaned over to help her. She closed her eyes again like they pained her and Tristan moved to sit next to her on the bed. He pulled her into his arms, needing to feel her warmth against him.

"I'm afraid you're still not making any sense to me. Have I missed something?"

"When your Aunts wanted me to know how to do the spells to save you, they imported their lifetime of knowledge into me magically and knocked me unconscious for four hours. It hurt like hell."

Tristan could imagine the scene, and it explained what had happened to his Aunts. He was glad they were with their mates but furious that they'd placed Ashlee in danger. She never should have been left alone to face the mystics. It was far too early. He swallowed down his temper. Nothing he could do about it now.

"So who keeps doing it to you? My Aunts?" He would get Ashlee to make sense.

"No, now it's your mother."

He narrowed his eyes to look at her before he massaged her neck. "Ashlee, I never saw you hit your head, but I think you must have. Maybe we should get your father back here to check you out again." He started to move when she grabbed his arm. "Your mother is waiting for your father. She wanted me to know how to bring back the women, how to restore the pack, so she imparted the knowledge and it knocked me on my behind again." Ashlee laughed and the sound filled him up. "I'm going to have to start being careful when I let people touch me. It really hurts my head when they do that."

He grinned at her. Her claim sounded impossible. His mother had been dead for years. Yet…why was it any less possible than all the other things they'd dealt with over the last thirty years? "Shall I enact a rule? No one wanting to dump information into Ashlee's brain may touch her without permission?"

She lowered her eyes for a moment and then raised them as she reached up to touch the side of his face. His heart stopped for a moment before it started pounding again. Just the touch of her hand on his skin was enough to bring him to his knees.

"Your eyes are still wolf." Her voice was little more than a whisper.

"They always will be now. It comes with the Alpha job." He paused, unsure how to continue. "Do you hate it?"

Ashlee shook her head. "Just have to get used to it. "

"Do you hate me?" And there was the question he had to have answered. He'd been out of his mind, crazed. Could she ever forgive him?

"Of course not. None of this was your fault. What a ridiculous question." Ashlee growled at him, loudly. He repressed the urge to crack up. His mate, who just a week ago hadn't even known she was a wolf now growled like a pro.

"I was worried."

Ashlee leaned over to kiss him and for a moment he stopped breathing, but as her lips pressed into his, he was reborn. Tentatively, he felt Ashlee's tongue pushed into his mouth where he gladly welcomed her. He'd almost lost everything, and then he'd been given more than he ever imagined possible. Never again would she be disappointed or hurt.

She pulled back and looked at him. "Are you still worried?"

He shook his head and kissed her again, angling his body to push her down on the bed. Tristan tried to tell himself to slow down, she'd been injured and exhausted but Ashlee seemed to want to move a frantic pace, and he was glad to oblige her. She pulled at his shirt and he threw it on the floor.

Feeling turnabout was fair play, he quickly took hers off too. She grinned at him. "Wow, for being the big Alpha, you still take direction pretty well." Her voice was teasing and he wanted to lick it up.

He kissed up and down her neck, stopping every once in a while to suck on a particularly sensitive area. "You called me Alpha out in the circle today. I don't want you to do that again. I'm your mate, that's how I want you to think of me."

"You're both, Tristan, and that's how it's supposed to be. In certain circumstances, I'm going to think of you as my Alpha. My wolf won't have it any other way. And—oh, I can't talk while you do that to me." He'd obviously hit on a spot she liked, so he spent a little extra time nuzzling it.

She sighed, and he was done talking. He drew her closer, needing her heat, demanding the connection between them. Her mouth was heaven to him, each press of her lips or small noise she made sent waves of pleasure through his body until he thought he might explode from it.

It was different this time. The few days they'd spent away from each other had made Ashlee more confident, more sure of herself and Tristan, who would have sworn he couldn't have been more attracted to Ashlee than he already was, fell even more under her spell as his love for her furthered his protective instincts. She was his. She'd kiss only him for the rest of her life. He was Alpha now, responsible for everyone and everything that happened to his pack. He was powerful, but she owned him. With one look, she could destroy him, and yet the woman who had been gifted to him seemed willing to forgive him for the horrible things he had done. He cherished her. Because of Ashlee, he could live with his burdens, as long as she kept kissing him like this.

His chest pressed against hers, he fiddled with the closure of her bra until she finally took pity on him and undid it herself. At the sight of her freed breasts, his groin strained painfully against his pants, but he would not rush. He would make it last for both of them.

Ashlee's mouth was so gentle beneath his, so soft. He worried the days-old growth of stubble on his face might irritate her soft skin, but when he tried to pull away, she pushed her face harder against him. Then all thoughts of gentleness faded. In the past when they had kissed, he had been able to differentiate the tastes of Ashlee, the flavors that made her who she was, but now his wolf roared inside of him that she tasted like his, like home, and Tristan had to agree.

Tristan pulled himself off his feeding frenzy on her mouth to kiss down her neck towards her stomach. His hands stroked the tender skin of her abdomen. He tongued her belly button and she laughed out loud.

He raised an eyebrow to look at her. "I'm amusing you?"

"Just ticklish."

He slid her pants down her legs and looked at her panties. He inhaled, his wolf senses telling him that she was as turned on as he was. Tristan closed his eyes at the scent. When he opened them, Ashlee's eyes had gone wolf.

"Think you're the only one who can do that?"

She reached out and cupped him through his pants and he almost lost it right there. He growled at her and pulled her panties down her legs.

She cocked an eyebrow at him as he leaned down to devour her soft, wet core. "Not that I'm complaining, Tristan, but I'm completely naked and you have your pants on." When his tongue tasted her sweetness she cried out and her head fell back against the pillows. He loved the way she tasted and he was happy to devote himself to his task. Her orgasm over took her and it was the most beautiful sight he'd ever witnessed.

He quickly shed his pants and his briefs, desperate to be inside of her heat. As the last tremors of her orgasm rocked her, he slid himself inside. It was heaven and for a moment, he closed his eyes and let himself enjoy the feel of being nestled inside of her. Ashlee lifted her hips and he was lost. She arched and he plunged, enjoying the dance, loving the rhythm until he spent himself inside of her in a moment of pure bliss, the likes of which he hadn't known was possible.

Careful not to hurt her, he withdrew from her and lay down on the bed, pulling her into his arms. She shivered gently, but her face, eyes closed, her mouth relaxed in a contented smile, told him she was happy and not injured in anyway. He leaned over to kiss the top of her head and inhaled the smell of their lovemaking.

Tristan let himself close his eyes and fall asleep.

Ashlee awoke later and judged from the angle of the sun that came through the window that it was morning. Where on earth was she? She looked around and decided that it had to be one of the abandoned cabins, based on the old wooden walls and the furniture that was clearly out of the 1970s, coupled with the orange shag rug,. It made sense. Where else would they be, considering that Tristan had burned down the Institute?

She rolled over to look at him. His eyes closed,

he looked peaceful and her heart jumped in delight. Tears filled her eyes. Perhaps she hadn't been the one to rescue him, he'd all but saved himself, but he was back and that was all that mattered.

He opened one eye to look at her. She swallowed hard. It was going to take some time to get used to the wolf eyes always being with her and truthfully, she would miss the depths of Tristan's human gaze.

She reached out to stroke his cheek. "We can't take you off this island if you're not wearing sun glasses."

He smiled and she leaned over to kiss his lips. He cleared his throat. "I know."

"Where are my parents?" She suddenly wondered if she should cover up in case they busted through the door.

Tristan sat up in bed, the lower half of his body covered by a thin sheet. Ashlee smiled, knowing quite well what hid beneath and thinking that in another moment she might grab him and start their fun again. "Well, Summer couldn't get out of here fast enough, she left with your parents several hours ago. I don't know how much you remember but she is clearly Cullen's mate."

Ashlee's mouth fell open in surprise. She hadn't seen that coming. "Oh, poor Cullen."

Tristan laughed out loud. "Your mother is somewhat freaked out because she has a rather difficult history with Cullen. She used to get in trouble all the time. She informed him in no uncertain terms that Summer will be finishing college over the next two years and he's to leave her alone. Cullen is so freaked out about having a mate he doesn't know which direction is up or down and he has disappeared to wherever he goes. In the meantime, your sister, who is terrified about her first shift—it was rather dramatic—has announced that she's not going to back to college, and that she intends to pursue a career in singing. This got your father all distraught and the three of them left in a huff about an hour before I moved you here, assured you would be fine."

Ashlee shook her head in disbelief. "Wow. Singing, really? Summer was always the one they thought would take after Dad and go to medical school."

"I've decided not to get involved in Cullen's mating issues. Its private; they will work it out eventually."

"So do you want to hear how we're going to bring back all the women?"

He nodded his head, "Absolutely."

"You're going to get really adept at using the architecture software."

He raised one eyebrow, one of the top ten looks Tristan gave, Ashlee decided.

"I am?"

"Yes and you're going to rebuild the institute in the next six months."

He shook his head. "That might be pushing things, winter's coming."

"You'll get it done." It wasn't a question, she was sure he would.

He shrugged. "Okay."

"Then you are going to consult with my parents about opening a resort on that island right over there." She pointed at the island two over from Westervelt. Tristan got up and crossed to the window to look out at it. "You're going to need to design and build that too."

He whirled around to look at her. "A lot of building going on here."

"It will be a huge success, my father will do surgeries there, we'll market it as a high-class private getaway where people can recover from their nips and tucks, like a spa. Dad's pretty famous in his profession, so I know people will come."

"Do you think we're going to bring the female shifters, their children, and mates back with promises of plastic surgery?"

Wasn't she being perfectly clear? Ashlee groaned. "Why would people who are eternally thirty need plastic surgery?"

Tristan choked on a laugh. "Being forever thirty does not guarantee beauty, little Ashlee."

Ashlee put her hands on her hips. "Some might come for the surgery, some might come for a vacation, some might come to work at the resort, but humans and shifters alike will all come because I'm going to place a spell on the advertisement."

"How can we be sure they'll see it?"

"We're going to run the ad everywhere and for a long time and eventually everyone who needs to see it, will see it."

Tristan moved to her and put his hands on her

shoulders. "This is a lot of building, are you sure this is going to work? Have you asked your father?"

"Yes to the first question, no to the second, but don't worry, he'll do it. I'm his Alpha's mate and his oldest daughter." Ashlee looked down for a second, not wanting to tell him the next part. "In the meantime, Gabriel and Michael can train the pack for the war that's coming, a war that will be harder for your father to conduct in plain sight of a major functioning resort."

Ashlee watched Tristan exhale his breath. "You think it's going to come to that? We won't get him before that happens?"

"I'm sorry Tristan, I blew our cover when I removed the witch from IPAG. There's no way it will ever be that easy again."

"We've placed your whole family in jeopardy, and your father is in the game now."

Ashlee nodded but didn't answer, she couldn't, it made her too ill to think about.

"Alright, little Ashlee, we'll get this started right away."

Ashlee shook her head and reached down to caress his groin. "Maybe not right away."

1 YEAR LATER

Ashlee clutched Braden close to her chest to block the wind from hitting him. He made a small gurgle noise and she pulled on his pumpkin costume to make sure it fit him snugly. Her eyes caught Tristan in the distance. She still automatically looked for him in a crowd. He stood, his dark sunglasses in place, and discussed the siding that the contractor was about to place on the Institute.

A cool wind blew behind them and not a second later, Tristan raised his head to look at her. He must have caught her scent. She smiled at him and kissed the head of their baby. With the exception of Braden, who had come as a surprise to them, everything was going just the way she'd planned it.

Tristan nodded to the men he stood with and crossed down the hill toward Ashlee. She grinned and raised her mouth for a kiss, which he gave her.

"Almost done?"

Tristan shrugged. "Another week, I think. Maybe two. How's our little pup?"

Ashlee laughed. "Sleeping because it's daytime. He'll be up all night again."

"I can stay up with him, if you want."

"Thanks for offering but that didn't go so well last time." Hearing nothing but commotion, Ashlee had arrived in Braden's room to find Tristan covered in spit-up holding Braden at arm's length as their son peed all over the wall.

"I'm a pro now, I've got a system."

Ashlee laughed and pulled him into her free arm. Kendrick might attack any day and they still had to complete the resort to bring back the pack's mates, but all of that would be worked out soon. Confidence filled her, she had her wolves. Both of them.

Mine.

No…Ours.

ABOUT THE AUTHOR

As a teenager, Rebecca would hide in her room to read her favorite romance novels when she was supposed to be doing her homework. She hopes that these days, her parents think it was worth it.

She is the mother of two adorable boys, with a third baby on the way, and she is fortunate to be married to her best friend. They live in northern New Jersey and try not to freeze too badly during the winter months.

A hardcore fan of science fiction, fantasy, and the paranormal, Rebecca tries to use all of these elements in her writing. She's been told she's a little bloodthirsty so she hopes that when you read her work you'll enjoy the action-packed ride that always ends in romance. In her world, anything is possible, anything can happen, and you should suspect it probably will.

Please visit
WWW.REBECCAROYCE.COM
or
WWW.REBECCAROYCE.BLOGSPOT.COM
for more information!

BOOKS BY REBECCA ROYCE

The Westervelt Wolves
Her Wolf
Summer's Wolf
Wolf Reborn
Wolf's Valentine
Wolf's Magic
Alpha Wolf

The Warrior
Initiation
Driven (coming soon)

The Conditioned
Eye Contact (coming soon)

Sexy Superheroes
Screwing the Superhero
Banging the Superhero

Outsiders
Love Beyond Time
Love Beyond Sanity
Love Beyond Loyalty

Other Works
First Dimension
Simon's Fate
Yes, Captain
Behind The Scenes